MISADVENTURES OF A VIRGIN

BY
MEREDITH WILD

MISADVENTURES
OF A
VIRGIN

BY
MEREDITH WILD

WATERHOUSE PRESS

For Cindy

Special thanks to Janny Kleine

CHAPTER ONE

Falls Edge has a way of making a person feel small. Human. A tiny speck between a majestic panorama of clouds and the valley floor. The mountains take up the middle ground and stare down on us— silent, imposing, arms wide in all their wonder. I've spent my life wrapped in these arms, year after year being a humble little speck, serving martinis and Old Fashioneds to the country's elite on the veranda that stretches from one end of the red-roofed Falls Edge Hotel to the other. And no matter how many women in pearls and white pants snip at me for this or that, all I can ever feel is blessed that of all places, this is where I call home.

Hundreds of thousands of patrons have passed through the hotel over the years. Presidents have lain in its beds. Captains of industry have graced its bars and ballrooms. And I've been working the veranda serving these patrons every summer since I turned thirteen and Daddy decided I needed to start being a part of the family business. Now I help him with the books, cover shifts between my classes at the local college, and put out fires on our busy weekends. I can't imagine doing it all on my own, but one day the hotel will be mine, the same way it was once my mother's.

For now, though, we're booked full and the veranda is at capacity. Every white wicker couch and lounge chair is occupied by an eager customer, and I'm doing all I can to keep up and smile while I do.

Pellegrino. Two glasses. Dirty martini. Straight up. No olives. Shirley Temple. Extra cherries.

I silently chant the last requests in my head as I pass through the wide double doors into Eve's, the bar named after the hotel's original owner.

"McCasker, what the *hell* are you doing here?" My father's tone is less than courteous.

I peek around the corner just as Edwin McCasker passes through the front doors. The old oak floors creak under his boots. Daddy circles the reception desk like he means to turn him around and send him back to the other side of the valley. But Edwin doesn't seem affected. He walks into the lobby, all dirty jeans and matching denim work shirt. His eyes are clever, a searing blue, and his smile has always melted any animosity my father would rather I hold toward him.

"Gerald Bell. Always a pleasure." Edwin nods in my direction and shoots me that smile. His hands are tucked casually into his jeans. "June."

I bite my lip to keep from returning his smile. Daddy stands in front of him, arms crossed as tightly as his navy blazer will allow. He's a few inches shorter and infinitely more high-strung than the man in front of him.

"I said, what are you doing here?" My father's tone is hushed now. No guests seem to have noticed his earlier outburst.

"I thought I'd stop by. See how the better half lives."

My father scoffs. "The better half. I've earned every dime and put damn near all of it back into making this a better place for our guests and our town. We're not fat and happy hogs up here. If you haven't noticed—and I know you haven't because you're an ignorant fool—that we're employing half the damn town here. No thanks to you."

Edwin's easy smile doesn't falter. "I feel like all these years we've just been misunderstanding each other, Ger."

"I feel like all these years you've been misunderstanding simple arithmetic, and if you'd get your head out of the clouds and see that rundown farm for what it is, a—"

"An impediment to you lining your wallet with a little bit more of Falls Edge tourist dollars. Am I right?"

"You're dead wrong, as usual. We both know it's a wasted opportunity to not expand on the one thing that keeps the tourists coming to our town. How many head of cattle you have there? They're doing nothing but stinking up the main road."

"Those stinking cows are my livelihood, Ger. We can't all be living a life of luxury like your guests."

"You could retire on the sale of the land, you idiot!"

My father's face is a fierce red. His arms, no longer crossed, are tight along his sides, ending in balled fists that I know he'd never use to hurt another human being. To my knowledge he's never been a violent man, but for some reason, I bet if he broke his streak, it'd be on Edwin McCasker.

I've only ever known the man as my father's worst enemy and lifelong rival. He also happens to be our neighbor. Over the past four years, my father has been trying to buy the McCasker land to develop an expansion of the hotel. At first Edwin had agreed, but once my father lined up the investors to fund the exchange, McCasker backed out.

Edwin looks through the windows that offer a view of the veranda and the majestic mountains beyond. "Pretty day."

My father wrinkles his brows. "It's more than a pretty day. It's a holiday weekend, and we're busy. Unless you're here to make good on the deal, you can turn on around and let us get back to work."

"I realize there's nothing you want more than to buy up the land like we talked about. The truth is, the decision isn't entirely mine. It never has been."

"Like hell it's not."

Edwin raises his hands in surrender. "Honest to God. I considered your offer, and I thought it was the best thing too. Then Kase left for school, and things changed. I realized that me making a decision for both of us wasn't really fair. He's entitled to have a say in his future."

The mere mention of Edwin's son has my heart beating faster.

"He's home now," I say quietly.

It's not a question, because I knew the day he stepped foot back in Falls Edge. Somehow I got wind of it every time he came home, even if he never stayed long enough for us to cross paths.

Edwin nods. "He's home, and he's here to stay. He wants to work the farm. Take over where I've fallen short. Turn it profitable again."

"Certainly he's got more sense than you do," my father says. "Send him up here. I'll explain everything. The benefits to the town and to your family are clear. You'd have a stake in the profits going forward."

Edwin's expression takes on a seriousness I've never seen before.

"I'm sure you could explain it very well. Doesn't change the fact that he's decided to keep the land in our family. It's his legacy too. I have to respect that."

"Nonsense!"

My father goes toward him, but I race up to his side.

"Daddy, wait. It's not his fault."

"Not his fault! You have no sway with the boy?"

"A bit, sure. But he's grown. He's seen a world beyond this valley, and I'm not about to tell him I know any better." His gaze flickers up to me. "I have a lot of faith in the next generation. It's a different world, a better world because of them. And it's his decision as much as it is mine now."

My father opens his mouth to speak again, but I start before he can.

"Mr. McCasker, if Kase wants to make Falls Edge his home, the expansion my father planned would ensure our town had a bright future. A future that could benefit him too. I'm sure he can see reason."

He's quiet a moment. "You know, June, he always liked you." He rubs his fingertips over the creases in his forehead.

Daddy's frown deepens. I'm holding my breath. Maybe because all this talk of Kase has me thinking about how his eighteen-year-old lips felt against mine all those years ago. The hotel sits on hundreds of acres of land, but the hidden grove where we stole a kiss and a few fevered touches under the stars is still my favorite spot.

One kiss. That's all I got before he left.

"Maybe you could talk to him. Hell, I've been wanting to bury this hatchet for years," Edwin says quietly.

My father grimaces, but I put my hand on the lapel of his blazer before he can speak.

"Daddy, why don't you let me show Edwin out. I'll just be a minute. I think someone may need your help at the front desk."

His grimace flattens into a friendlier customer-service expression once he notices a young couple waiting to check out. He gives me a short nod and walks briskly toward them. A wave of relief forces me to exhale. I gesture toward the door, and Edwin and I move side by side onto the wide front porch.

Our valet, Marty, tips his hat as we pass. I recognize Edwin's truck parked down the narrow winding drive. It's an old, white Chevy pickup with McCasker Farms painted in faded blue lettering on the doors.

"I appreciate you coming by," I say.

He shoots me a crooked grin that I'm certain Kase inherited. "Not sure your daddy shares your appreciation."

"He's not always an easy man to deal with, but he means well. I can assure you his heart is in the right place."

Edwin sighs and stares ahead. The crisp dusky air willows over us. "I sure hope so. That land has been in my family for five generations. No part of giving it up would be easy."

We slow as we near his truck. He takes out his keys, bouncing them in his callused palms a few times before making eye contact.

"You really think the expansion would be good for Falls Edge? For our family?"

I see years of hard work on his face, in the lean but tired muscles that fill out his work clothes. And I see equal measures of doubt and hope in his eyes.

"I do," I say. I mean it. I've seen the numbers, and I've watched the demand for accommodations in our little mountain town steadily grow over the years. "My mother put everything she had into keeping the hotel going through every downturn. I'm committed to doing what's best, the same way she would have."

Edwin purses his lips and looks down at his boots. "Your mother was a very special woman. Hard worker with an incredible heart. She made everyone around her a better person."

A heavy silence passes between us, and I almost ask him about her. My father never says much. I suspect he's been brokenhearted since she died when I was a baby. Still, I savor every tidbit I can get to somehow know her better. Then Edwin looks up, and something about his expression gives me pause. I recognize the heartache there before he softens with a smile.

"I meant what I said about Kase. You should talk to him."

I swallow hard. "Do you think he would...you know... reconsider?"

Edwin reaches in the truck, smooths back his golden-brown hair with his other hand, and tugs on a hat that bears the same McCasker Farms logo. "Come by tonight. He's been working himself into the ground since he got home. Would be a healthy distraction for him in any case."

I offer a tentative nod, but the prospect of seeing Kase has already set off a cyclone of nerves and anxiety in my belly. He hasn't sought me out for four years. Why would he want to see me now?

Before I can come up with an excuse to back out, Edwin's in the driver's seat, slamming the heavy door behind him. He winks at me through the window and sets off down the long drive toward the main road.

CHAPTER TWO

I finish my shift, convince Daddy that a trip to see Kase is the only chance we may have to buy the land, and agonize for another hour over what to wear. With the heat wave we're having, my options are limited. Eventually I throw on some white shorts and a simple tank top. After all, this isn't a date. This is business, pure and simple.

I remind myself of this repeatedly during the three-minute drive from the hotel lot to the McCasker farmhouse. I haven't seen Kase in four years. No contact. No hint that our moment together meant anything to him. The last thing I want is to give him the impression that I give a damn about it either. That kiss and the way his roaming hands felt on me are ancient history.

I park and check my reflection in the rearview mirror. My sandy-brown hair is tied back in a ponytail, and my bangs fringe my face. My mascara hasn't melted in the heat, and a light coat of lip gloss shimmers on my lips. I could have gone totally natural, but the truth is, no matter what I tell myself, I do care.

I scold myself for that fact and exit my Jeep, giving the door a good hard slam before I ascend the stairs to the front porch. The door opens before I can knock, leaving only the rickety old screen door between Edwin and me before he opens that too.

He melts my uncertainty with a smile. "June, come on in. I'll get

Kase. He's been in the barn all day."

I step inside. "If it's not a good time, I could come back later."

"Nonsense. He needs to hang it up for the day anyhow."

He leaves me in the kitchen, and I hear the back door squeak open and slam shut.

"Kase!" Edwin shouts out toward the field and the barn that sits in the back.

As the seconds tick by, I take in the interior of the house. The first floor is cut up into four areas—a kitchen, dining room, den, and a narrow staircase that leads to the second floor. It's a decent-sized home, but the layout gives the house a traditional, poky feel. The wood floors need refinishing. The paint on the walls is dull and dated. As far as I can tell, nothing but country breeze cools the first floor. The McCasker farmhouse has a roof and four walls but lacks the charm and luxury I'm used to at the hotel.

I hear my father's voice in my head and faintly regret that I can see his point. There's not much here I would cherish so much not to sell. Then again, not many people were raised in a four-star hotel.

"What are you grinning about?"

The sound carries through the screen door. Those five little words and knowing Kase uttered them does something to me instantly. I stop my perusal of the house and stare at Edwin's back blocking my view. Kase is only a few feet away. My mind races to imagine what he looks like now. How has he changed? If only Edwin would move aside so I could see him...

"June is here to see you," Edwin says.

"June?"

My heart pangs with disappointment. He doesn't remember

me. He doesn't remember...

"June Bell... Ring a bell? I saw her at the hotel today. Told her to stop by."

"What the hell did you do that for?"

The frustration in his tone is unmistakable, and now I feel it too. The tempo of my heart picks up for reasons altogether different now.

"Kase, you haven't exactly been a social butterfly since you got home. Didn't figure it'd hurt to spend time with someone other than me."

"Goddamnit." Kase mutters the curse low, and his voice drifts away slowly.

My girlish anxiety over seeing him again has taken a sharp turn. Years of wishing for something more, for *anything*, funnels into a blinding indignation.

Edwin turns back and finds me in the kitchen. He's shaking his head and avoiding my gaze. "That boy is something else. I'm sorry, June."

I can't find the right words, and his father doesn't deserve my anger. I should go. No way he's going to agree to sell the land, with or without Kase's blessing. But if I accept that and walk away now, the whole thing is a waste. If this is the end of the road with the McCaskers, I decide now it's going to be on my terms.

I walk around Edwin and march out onto the back porch. Kase's figure is already small in the distance, rounding the barn. I could call after him, but if he kept walking away, I'm not sure my heart would ever recover.

I follow his path. The grass in the field is overgrown and brushes against my calves. The sun is melting into the horizon, but the air is thick with summer and the smells of the farm—meadow flowers, grass, and the dairy cows that graze nearby.

I hear a loud splash just as I retrace his journey around the barn. I stop at the bank of the creek that runs along the south side of the property. Kase's clothes and boots are in a heap a couple feet away. All the fiery words I planned to throw at him get stuck in my throat when I see him with water up to his waist.

I shouldn't be here. A voice in my head tells me to leave. Still, I can't seem to move. He hasn't seen me yet, and I'm riveted to the man before me. His back is broad and muscular. No doubt, he's a far cry from the lean boy who'd tempted my teenaged heart.

He dunks under, and when he rises again, he strokes his fingers through his damp hair, sending rivulets of water down his back. Good God.

Then he turns. Our eyes lock. My mouth is dry, and once again I'm searching for words. His features are more chiseled than I remember. Golden stubble covers the strong line of his jaw. His cheekbones are more defined. His eyes are still a vibrant blue, like the clearest summer sky.

I don't know how the hell I feel about this man one minute to the next. All I know is that if he weren't Kase McCasker, the one who barely knows my name, I'd be searching for reasons to stay and get to know him better.

"Sorry. I'll go." My voice is strangled and awkward. I turn to leave, shaking my head as I go.

"June, wait."

I whip back. "Oh, now you know my name?"

He frowns. "What the hell does that mean?"

"Really?" I glare down at him, unable to hold back any longer. "You didn't seem to a minute ago. Then again, it's been four years. Not sure why you'd remember me. Not like I mattered enough to see even once when you came home."

His lips tighten, but his eyes bore into me with an intensity I'm not ready for.

I'm mad, but I'm hurt more. I'm ready for a fight, but all I really want is...

What do I want? An apology? Acknowledgment that he wanted me as much as I wanted him, even for a fleeting moment?

"I just thought after that night..." My tone is softer now.

"I remember everything, June."

I shake my head. "You just walked away from me like the sound of my name hurt to hear."

"It does, but not for the reasons you think. And I wasn't walking away from you."

"Really? Sure looked like you were walking away. Awfully fast too."

"Jesus, June, give me a break. I smell like a barn." He points to the pile of clothes at my feet. "No one told me you were coming by. You think I wanted to see you that way?"

Feeling less justified in my anger, I drop my hand from my hip. "Sorry. I just... I should go."

I turn to leave again, and this time his voice doesn't stop me. I cross the field quickly, but I don't go back through the house. Cutting through the side yard, I'm nearly at my Jeep when I hear Kase behind me.

"June, wait."

When I turn, my jaw goes slack. He was a sight in the creek moments ago. But this close...

He's still drenched, shirtless, his jeans zipped but unbuttoned and his boots unlaced like he'd thrown on just enough to chase after me. I ball my hands into fists to keep from reaching for him and sliding my fingers through his damp hair. His chest moves under quick breaths. It's irrational, but I want to touch him everywhere. Over his shoulders. Down his wet pectorals. Hell, every ridge of his abdomen is permanently imprinted on my mind now.

"Damn..." His voice is a physical rasp against my skin.

I flicker my gaze back up to his. His lips are parted as his eyes search mine.

"What?" I unball my fists and rub them down the sides of my shorts, suddenly nervous that he's seeing me this close up now too.

He shakes his head slightly. "Four years, huh?"

"Four years, Kase. And not a word."

"I had my reasons."

"You made me feel like I meant something to you. What reasons did you have for not breathing a word to me since then?"

"For God's sake, you were sixteen. We were just kids. What was I supposed to do?"

I swallow over my hurt pride, but I feel what I feel. I refuse to believe that even my teenaged brain overestimated the power of the moment we shared.

"I was old enough to kiss. Old enough for you to put your hands on me like you did. Old enough to make me want a lot more."

He exhales shakily but takes a solid step toward me. His tone is low when he speaks again. "Believe me, that kiss wasn't anything close to what I wanted to do to you."

A rush of heat simmers under my skin with his admission. How many times had I fantasized about that night at the falls? How many times had I tried to imagine what it would have felt like to give myself to him?

"Well, it's too late now," I whisper, not trusting my voice not to waver. I stare down at the overgrown grass between us. "I came here to talk about the land. That's all."

He's quiet a moment. "What about the land?"

"Sounds like your dad is open to selling again, but he says it's up to you. Now that you're home, I came to talk some sense into you."

A heavy silence falls between us. When I meet his eyes again, my heart slams against my chest. How can one man have this kind of power over me? He's a crush, and I'm woman enough to know how ridiculous it is to feel this way.

"Forget it. I shouldn't have come," I say.

I pull my keys from my pocket, but he snatches them from me. I move to snatch them back but hesitate. Determination lines his jaw and defines the already taut lines of his frame.

"Give me my keys. You obviously don't want me here."

He doesn't budge. "What did you mean when you said it's too late?"

I frown. "What?"

"You just said it was too late. Who are you seeing?"

"I'm not seeing anyone. Not that it's any of your damn business."

He doesn't look satisfied with that answer. "Then who..." He swallows and looks away a moment. "Who were you with after I left?"

My lips part, because I'm lost. Why would he suddenly care?

"What are you asking me? I wasn't *with* anyone." Heaven knows, if I had been, I could have stopped obsessing about the possibility of being with Kase. Could have stopped hoping we would pick up where we left off when he came home from school on breaks. But, no, I had been foolishly committed to the fantasy of him, the promise of what we could be.

Somehow Kase looks as lost as I feel. "You haven't been with anyone since I left?"

I shrug. "Not really, no." I'd had a few casual dates, but I'd known everyone in this town since I was in diapers. If someone was going to turn my head, they would have long ago.

"So... You're saying..."

I huff and reach for my keys again, but he holds them out of reach. "Jesus, Kase. Spit it out or let me go home."

"Are you still a virgin?"

My cheeks heat fiercely, and it has nothing to do with the summer night falling all around us. I stop reaching for the keys and stare into his eyes. I'm not sure how I feel. Embarrassed, because I haven't gotten around to finding someone to hold my interest long enough to take me to bed. Angry, because after four years this is all Kase seems to care about. Shamefully aroused, because after four years this is all Kase seems to care about...

He lifts his empty hand, brushing his thumb over the contour of my cheek. My heart wants to explode at his touch.

"I wanted you, June. You can't possibly know how much," he says softly. "I had no idea you'd wait for me."

Everything inside me is rioting. My thoughts, scattered with unspoken desires. My blood stream, pumping hard with adrenaline from being this close to him again. My emotions, pinging around like the sixteen-year-old virgin he put under his spell. It's too much. I can't let him do this to me. Not after years of nothing.

I brush his hand away brusquely.

"Get over yourself, Kase. I wasn't *waiting* for you." I wish it were true, but it feels like a lie. "You think I spent all this time gazing up at the stars wondering why you didn't take my virginity when you had the chance? While you were in college having your fun, I was here working, doing everything I could to keep the hotel running, which, if you didn't already know, keeps half the town running. That's why we need to talk about the land."

His stare is unwavering and intense. He's gripping my keys so hard his knuckles are white. "You're lying to me."

I prepare to convince him otherwise, but before I can, he curls his hand at my nape and tugs me toward him. Our lips are a breath apart.

"I'm not lying."

"Kiss me, and I'll prove you wrong." His voice is gravel, and the demand makes my knees weak.

Damn him.

"Go to hell," I mutter.

A second later our mouths are sealed. I'm hauled against his hard, wet body, and then we stumble together until my back meets the Jeep. The keys hit the ground with a clang, and his hands slide across my cheeks. He cradles my face while our lips reacquaint.

He's exactly as I remember. Soft yet demanding. When he licks into my mouth, I open and welcome the rush of his flavor.

"God, I missed this," he whispers against my lips before stealing another greedy kiss.

My hands are trembling when I finally reach for him. His chest is cool to the touch. Wet and soft under my palms. My touch seems to release his. He skims his palms down my neck and over my aching breasts, squeezing gently before settling low on my hips.

Every caress makes me crave more. As if answering my silent plea, he lowers one hand between my legs.

"Kase." I whimper against his lips, because I need him to take mercy on me. I can't take much more of this.

Then he palms my mound possessively. The heat and pressure against the pulsing need between my thighs is almost more than I can bear.

"Mark my words, June. This is mine."

I can't breathe. Can't speak. He resolves both by taking my mouth again. Taking more, demanding more.

This is mine.

His claim echoes through me over and over. My limbs hum like the prongs on a tuning fork. I'm light-headed, falling into this kiss and welcoming every bold touch like we never have to stop. It's as if I've waited all this time to hear those words and offer him every last inch of my body.

He strokes his tongue against mine in perfect time to the tantalizing slide of his palm up and down the front of my shorts. I moan into his mouth, claw back my self-control, and will my body not to arch into his touch.

I need to think. I can't think with him this damn close to me.

I press against his chest, but he's got me pinned. I turn my head to break the kiss, and his lips go right to my neck.

I have to stop this before I give him everything. All of me.

He nibbles my earlobe. "Mine," he whispers.

"No." I suck in a sobering breath, but my head's still buzzing. I turn to meet his gaze. "It's mine. And I'll give it to whoever I want."

His gaze is molten, and his golden skin is flushed. "Like hell you will."

"You had your chance."

I add some pressure against his chest. He pulls back a fraction, but his fingers are tucked into the band of my shorts now, tethering me to him.

"Don't challenge me, June. I never back down." His gaze darkens, and he licks his swollen lips.

My brain short-circuits. I'm suddenly not sure of anything. Why I pushed him away. Why I'm not letting him drag me to his room and plunder my body right here and now.

"You want this land?"

I blink a few times. "What?"

"That's why you came here, right? You want me to give Edwin the okay to sell off the land."

The world outside our immediate bubble slowly comes back into focus. My life. My responsibilities. To my father and the town and the legacy my mother would want me to carry on.

"Yes," I say simply. That's at least one of the reasons that brought me to his doorstep.

He takes a small step back, withdrawing his touch with it. I brace myself against the vehicle. I'm not sure I could stand without it. I welcome the space to think, but all I can seem to think about is when I'll feel him against me again.

"I'll agree to sign it over," he says quietly.

"You will?"

He nods wordlessly, dragging his fingertips through his damp hair. "One condition." He purses his lips slightly. "Maybe two."

I hesitate, my mind reeling. "What are the conditions?"

"Stay with me." The heat in his eyes is unmistakable. "Stay here with me before they tear it all down. Let me make up for the time we lost."

I stare at him in disbelief. Is he serious?

"Are you seriously trying to negotiate the land...for my virginity?"

He grins and trails his tongue along his lower lip. I should be outraged, but something clenches deep in my core.

"If you're asking me if I want to be the first one to push into that beautiful body, the answer is you're goddamn right. But I want a whole lot more than that."

"You're crazy," I mumble, but the sentiment seems to get lost with the merciful breeze blowing through the valley. The tiger lilies lining the path to the front door sway gently.

He closes the space between us again, brushing back a strand of hair that loosened from my ponytail. Lowering slowly, he presses a chaste kiss at the corner of my lips. "I'm getting a second chance, and I'm not letting you go this time. If that makes me crazy, so be it."

CHAPTER THREE

I left Kase and his ridiculous offer in the dust last night. Literally.

I sped away from his house with shaking hands and a racing heart, in utter disbelief that I still matter at all to him—and more, that he would offer up his family's land to have more of me.

He was the last thought before I drifted off to sleep and the first when I woke at dawn. Without a doubt, the night was filled more with tortured thoughts of Kase than restful sleep. I tossed and turned for an hour, but in the end, all I could do was get up and throw myself into another busy day and try to put him out of my mind.

The valley shimmers under a perfect cloudless day as I set up my station on the veranda. Guests are already scattered across the lawn and milling around the hotel sitting areas. Couples, families, and staff make every day a nonstop event. Today, I'm grateful for the distractions more than ever. If I spend one more minute mentally replaying Kase's indecent touches, I'm going to lose my damn mind.

I spot a young couple in my section eyeing the menu and walk over to them. "Can I get you two anything?"

The woman smiles. "Can I have a glass of chardonnay?"

"A Tuckerman's for me," her male counterpart says as he sits back and drapes an arm around her shoulder.

The princess-cut diamond on her left hand winks in the

sunlight. Judging from their apparent bliss, I'd be willing to bet they're newlyweds. Maybe even honeymooners. An unexpected pang of resentment hits me, but I force a smile.

"No problem. I'll be right back with those."

I spin and head inside to Eve's. Our bartender, Julie, is posted behind the little bar that services the veranda waitstaff and guests inside the hotel.

She waves as I approach. "Hey, girl."

"Hey," I say. "Chardonnay and a Tuckerman's, please."

She cocks her head, and her blond braid whips over her shoulder. "How about, 'Hey, how are you doing, Julie?' And then I'll say, 'Wiped out. I had to close down Mackie's last night.'"

I smile weakly. "Sorry. I'm a little out of it this morning."

"Tell me about it. You seem a million miles away."

"I didn't sleep great," I say. It's not a lie, but I have no interest in elaborating on how Kase McCasker has hijacked my brain and most of my body over the last twenty-four hours. "How are you doing?"

She reaches for a wine glass on the rack above the bar. "Wiped out. I had to close down Mackie's last night."

I laugh. "That sucks. Was it packed?"

"Wall to wall. The tourists are driving people to drink. Unfortunately, I'm not one of them. I'm working double shifts all week."

Unless helping my father run the hotel counts, I'm one of the few people in Falls Edge who works only one job. Julie is like most, serving drinks to the hotel guests by day and getting the locals drunk at the town's hole-in-the-wall bar by night. I don't envy her, but we all do what we must to get by in this little town. And Fourth-of-Julyweekend tips get most of us by.

"You should come by tonight after work. I'll buy you a drink." She sets the chardonnay and draft on my tray on the bar.

"Maybe."

She smirks. "You always say that."

She's tried getting me to Mackie's more than once, but I usually find a reason to bail. Julie's nice, but our time together usually consists of me counseling her through her latest fling until she sets her sights on a new one. Then again, I could probably use a stiff drink and a dose of someone else's problems to get Kase out of my head for a little while.

"Working hard?"

A set of tan, muscled arms rests on the bar beside me. The man they belong to knocks the wind out of me with his familiar heart-stopping grin. Kase is fully clothed this time, but that doesn't seem to lessen his effect on me. Unfortunately he's the only human I've ever met who can obliterate my brain cells with a look.

"Kase." I take in a breath but my lungs aren't expanding the way they're supposed to. "What are you doing here?"

He turns so his body faces me, one arm propped against the bar. Today he doesn't look like a man who works a farm. He looks like a normal college kid, in khaki cargo shorts, a plain white T-shirt, and sandals.

"I took the afternoon off. Thought I'd come see you. Finish that little chat we started last night."

In a flash, my cheeks are burning hot. I wish he couldn't see it, but I'm certain he does. "That conversation is over," I snap and look away.

His eyes are my weakness. They seem to sear right into my soul and see things other people don't see. It's impossible, yet I've believed it since we were kids. Ever since our fathers drew a line between our lives that was only crossed by circumstance. Passing each other in the halls of school. Ending up at the same friend's party. A glance here or there, but nothing like that night at the falls when that line suddenly didn't exist anymore.

"You going to at least buy me a cold drink?"

I sigh and get ready to tell him to buy his own damn drink, when we're interrupted.

"I'll buy you a drink. Angel's Envy on the rocks, right?"

For the first time since Kase showed up, I'm aware of Julie's presence. Kase glances toward her but doesn't meet her flirty smirk. His expression is empty, unreadable.

"I'm good. Thanks."

Julie leans in, hands wide on the bar and chest pushed out for Kase's benefit, no doubt. "I haven't seen much of you lately. How long have you been back?"

"A few weeks," he says flatly, returning his attention to me. "Now about that chat."

"Huh." Unaffected by Kase's obvious disinterest, Julie chews on her lip and gives him a thorough once-over. "You should come to Mackie's tonight. I'm working the bar."

I balance the tray on my palm and turn away so Julie can't see me roll my eyes. I can't take a second more of her shameless flirting, and my customers are waiting. I head toward them without another word, cursing her inwardly. No doubt she would take Kase to bed in a heartbeat, but the thought of having to counsel her through that one makes me feel homicidal. She can sleep through half the town, but Kase McCasker is off limits. I'm sure he's been with other people, but I'd rather endure torture than hear about it.

"Here you go. Let me know if you need anything else." I place the drinks in front of the young couple, and they thank me.

When I turn, Kase is settling into an empty chair in my section.

I walk over, hand on my hip. "My father won't be happy you're here, you know."

He sits back casually and stretches his legs out, crossing them at the ankle. "On the contrary, he seemed pretty happy to see me."

I pause. "Did you talk to him about selling the land?"

"I did. I think we have an understanding." His gaze glides over the panorama.

Now I want his eyes on me. I want the truth. "What understanding? What did you tell him?"

"Same thing I told you. He gets what he wants if I get what I want."

"What?" My voice is nearly a shriek. I'm certain all the blood has left my face. He couldn't have told my father about his offer. He must be joking, trying to rile me up.

Then he shifts his focus to me. "You spend two weeks at the farmhouse with me, and Edwin will sign on the dotted line to sell him the land just like they talked about years ago. Same deal. That gives him enough time to line up his investors again, and it gives me time to do what I need to do."

"What exactly is that?"

He hesitates a second. "I think I made my intentions pretty clear last night, don't you?"

The heat in his stare threatens to knock me on my ass. That confusing flood of emotions crashes over me again. I'm somewhere between outrage and desire, but I'm no doubt blushing like a schoolgirl.

"My father may want that land more than anything, but that's not enough to make him barter his daughter's virginity. If that's what you proposed to him, I'd suggest you find a safe place behind a locked door. He does own guns."

He chuckles. "I may be determined, but I'm not stupid. All he knows is that I want you to spend some time on the property before we turn it over. Your father may think it all amounts to a trash heap, but the land and everything on it will be yours eventually. You want to build on your family's legacy, right?"

"Of course," I say.

"Then it's only fair that you spend a little time recognizing mine before you make the call about what stays and what gets bulldozed in the name of expansion."

He uses air quotes when he says "expansion." As much as I know the plan to expand the hotel's accommodations and grounds is a smart one, I can't ignore the twinge of guilt I feel.

"You don't have to do this," I say.

He rises slowly and comes to me. We're only a few feet apart. I can feel his heat even from this distance.

"The decision's been made on my end. I'm just waiting on you, June."

I fold my arms tightly across my chest. Maybe to keep from touching him. Maybe to deter him from touching me and destroying all sense of reason—something I seem to have a lot less of lately.

"How do I know you'll honor your agreement? What if you take what you want and back out like your dad did?"

"I already put it in writing along with Edwin. Ask your father. He seemed satisfied with the terms."

We stand that way for a few silent seconds as I contemplate his proposal and how I can possibly agree to it.

"You're really serious about this," I finally say. "You're ready to sell the property if I do this?"

A small smile curves his lips. "Let's just say that seeing you again brought things into focus for me."

"What will you do after?"

He shrugs. "Never know where the future will take us."

I sigh and stare out at the mountains. They're silent, like gods of stone, offering no help in my current predicament.

"What do you say, June?"

I turn back. "One week."

He shakes his head. "Two. It's a big piece of property. If you need space, you'll have plenty of it. I still have my work to do, so you'll have your days to yourself. Your nights belong to me."

"I'm already scheduled for shifts here—"

"It's taken care of. Your father will make arrangements for your absence from the hotel for the next two weeks, starting tomorrow. No shifts on the veranda. No emergencies you need to attend to. Anything like that voids the agreement. The next fourteen days are mine, and I plan to take full advantage of them. I just need an answer. Yes or no."

I swallow hard. "What if I say no?"

An irrational fear spikes through me as I contemplate that.

What if I turn him down and another four years goes by without him in my life? What if yesterday's temptations become the last, a fresh set of memories to agonize over until I can find someone to make me forget him?

He reaches up and traces my lower lip. "Don't say no."

How can I? Have I ever wanted anything or anyone more than Kase?

"Fine." I exhale a shaky breath and unfold my arms. "I just have one condition of my own."

He barely masks a grin. Sunlight seems to dance in his blue eyes. "What is that?"

"We don't do...*that*...until I'm ready."

He's eerily silent so I keep on.

"I just don't want to feel pressured and ruin the moment. I want it to be good. I mean, for both of us obviously. What I'm saying is..." I gesture awkwardly and avoid his penetrating gaze. How can negotiating about how and when I lose my virginity be anything but awkward? "I just want to have a say in it, okay?"

A few tense seconds pass, but I press my lips together tightly to avoid spilling more of my fears.

"Look at me, June."

I look up as he leans in, close enough to threaten the last of my defenses.

"When I fuck you," his voice is low, lighting a fire under my skin, "you'll have more than a say in it. You're going to beg for it. And if you don't want to share my bed every night we're together after that, then I've been wrong about us from the start."

I have to fight to keep my legs under me. My chest heaves with short, quick breaths. How can he do that to me? Whip me up and turn me into putty in a matter of seconds?

"But if that's your only condition," he says, "I accept it. Now do we have a deal?"

I give him a slight nod.

"Say it," he murmurs quietly.

"We have a deal."

CHAPTER FOUR

The next few hours pass in a blur. Every time I let myself think about what I've agreed to, I screw up someone's order. So I don't. I work to the end of my shift and go look for my father. He's in his office, a grin curling his lips and the phone pressed to his ear.

"Yes, just as we discussed before. We could be ready to break ground in less than a month. There's nothing to do but prep the land." He pauses, unaware of my eavesdropping. "Perfect. I look forward to hearing back from you."

He hangs up, his smile wider as I step through the doorway and finally get his attention.

"Hey, Daddy."

He shoots up in his chair and claps his hands loudly. "Can you believe it, Junebug? They're really doing it."

His eyes are bright and his skin is flushed. His aura practically glows with hard-won satisfaction. I do my best to match his enthusiasm, but the rivalry with Edwin belongs to him, not me.

"I know. It is hard to believe," I say.

Hard to believe I'm doing this. Hard to believe that in a matter of days—hell, maybe hours—I'll be in Kase's bed, letting him do whatever unspeakable things he has in mind for our time together.

"Are you sure about this, Daddy?"

He freezes. "What do you mean? What's wrong?"

I avert my eyes, as if maybe he can somehow read the truth in them. "I mean, is it worth me being away from the hotel? I've never taken this kind of time off before."

"Oh." He waves his hand and drops down into his chair again. "That's no problem. We'll make it work. And anyway, I'll get to put Edwin to work. Won't that be fun!" He laughs heartily. "I should make him start with the bathrooms. Would serve him right for keeping us hanging like that all those years."

I frown. "You're putting him to work?"

"Well, see, that's one of the conditions Kase stipulated. He said half the reason he's agreeing to the sale is because Edwin can't shoulder the work of the farm anymore, not even with Kase helping him now. He wants me to spend the next couple weeks showing him the ropes here at the hotel. Thinks maybe he could be helpful with maintenance and odd things that come up."

"You're going to hire him?" My eyes go wide at the thought. Two sworn enemies sharing a workplace sounds like a disaster in the making.

He shrugs. "Who knows. Hell, I may not be able to get him to lift a finger. He's staying here on the pretense of a much-needed vacation. I'd rather toss him out on his can than look at him, but if it means getting this sale to happen, I'll play along."

He wags his eyebrows, and I almost laugh. I haven't seen him this happy, well, possibly ever.

Maybe I didn't give Kase enough credit. Bringing Edwin to the hotel was a clever move to keep him out of the farmhouse while I'm there. But it's also a chance to bury the hatchet on their rivalry once and for all. Still, they were at odds before the land sale fell through. I can't imagine two weeks will unwind the years of hatred between them.

"If something goes wrong, I can't come back. You know that, right?"

My father looks serious for a moment. "I know. I've relied on you here for as long as I can remember, June. I don't thank you enough for all you do."

If he only knew what I would do for the family business...

"Thanks, Daddy."

His phone rings again suddenly. "Oh, that's probably one of the investors. You'd better go pack. Don't worry about things here. We'll have it covered, all right?"

Before I can answer, he's back on the phone. "Hello? Hanson! Great to hear from you."

I turn and close the door behind me as my father prattles on about the merits of the expansion. I move in a daze to the service elevator that takes me to the fourth floor, where my father and I reside in our off hours. I unlock the door, throw off my apron, and drop onto my bed, the drama of the day heavy on me.

I look around, taking in the familiar luxuries I've grown used to—the fancy damask wallpaper, the slick dark-wood furniture, and the windows that offer a famous view of the mountains. Instead of a room in a house, I've gone to sleep here every night for as long as I can remember. My father's suite mirrors mine—a space that's more like a studio apartment with its own small sitting area, kitchenette, and bathroom. Simple and tidy, thanks to our cleaning staff and a life consumed by matters four floors down and everything in between.

I'm not sure if this is what my mother envisioned when she had me. Regardless, this is where I am. I've only ever known this world, and I'm about to be introduced to Kase's very soon.

I graze my hand over the bedspread, enjoying the way the silky fabric feels under my fingertips. I wonder what Kase's room will be like. If I'll like it. If I'll care or even notice what it looks like when he has his hands on me.

I shake my head with a sigh, hoping to dislodge the thought the way I've tried to at least a hundred other times today. I glance to my bureau, instantly overwhelmed with the prospect of packing. I don't even own a suitcase.

I go to the door that adjoins my room with my father's and head for his closet. I dig past boxes and some piles of saved newspapers until I find a leather suitcase. It's old and musty and nothing like the kind our guests travel with, but it'll have to do. I flip the latches to find it filled with more papers. Carefully, I lift them onto another pile and bring the suitcase to my room to begin the inevitable.

Thoughtful of the number of nights I'll spend away, I assemble a large pile of clothes and a few basic toiletries. As I begin arranging them in the suitcase, my fingers graze something tucked into an interior pocket. It's a photo, faded and curled from age. It shows four young people—two women and two men—in their swimsuits standing in front of a waterfall. I bring my face closer and try to discern who they might be.

One undoubtedly is my father, with his dark hair and light-green eyes that match mine. His arm is draped around another woman. She's pretty but looks nothing like my mother, who's standing on the other side of my father. Another handsome man leans toward her, his hand casually hanging over her shoulder.

I stare longer and harder. I turn it over. Champagne Falls is written there in black handwriting. I turn it back and recognize the details in the background. Then I recognize something else.

"Oh God," I whisper.

The other man by my mother's side is a much younger Edwin McCasker. A closer look reveals her arm around his waist, their smiles soft and broad. Like two people who care for each other. Like two people who might be more than good friends.

I tuck the photo back into the pocket hastily, as if my father might appear at any moment and discover what I've seen. What would he say? How would he explain why Kase's father knew my mother well enough to be photographed with her like this?

I go to the window and wrap my arms around my middle. The silhouette of the hotel casts a shadow over the back of the property. The darkness creeps gradually toward the base of the mountains as daylight recedes to the west.

For years I've longed to know more about Juliette Bell, the woman who gave me life before tragically losing hers. One night, after working late at the hotel, she'd been driving back to the country house her family shared with her, my father, and me as an infant. The roads were icy, and another driver coming around a curve on one of the treacherous mountain roads hit her head-on. That's all my father would say. For years I cautiously pried for more, only to be given short, irritated answers—or worse, ignored.

A sudden rush of anger overtakes my curiosity. I know more about the ways my father despises Edwin than I know about my own mother. Why? Today's not the day to ask, but I'm determined now in a way I haven't been before. If only Edwin were staying at the farmhouse while I was, I could ask him. I'd have to get him alone another time.

No less unsettled, I return to the case. I pluck the photo from its pocket to stare at it once more before tucking it back and finishing the task of packing. Anxiety about tomorrow and whatever the next two weeks will bring hits me every now and then, but the restless night and long day are slowly wearing me down.

I finish packing, change into pajamas, and nestle under the covers. As the minutes on the clock tick by, I wait for sleep to drown out my spinning thoughts. Instead of surrendering to my dreams, my mind drifts to the photo of my young mother, father, and Edwin. Like in the photo, she's been a phantom presence in my life, existing in her own quiet way. I've spent the past few years accepting her dreams as my own without question. What would I give for a day with her? An hour? A glimmer of a moment to know her better?

The air-conditioning kicks on, and for a minute, I imagine the sound is the steady rush of the falls, one of the many natural wonders here. An endless stream of mountain water crashing over a rocky ledge and onto dozens of smooth granite boulders, creating little pools perfect for wading.

I'd always been drawn to Champagne Falls for its peaceful magic, until one night when I was drawn there with Kase.

He'd been celebrating with the rest of the graduating class at a reception at the hotel. I worked the event, as I typically did. As the night came to a close, some of our friends who were looking for ways to keep the party going convinced us to break away from the rest of the group. We stole a few bottles of wine and ended up at a grove near the falls, passing around the libations and laughing at old stories and new gossip from the night.

The longer we stayed, the more I sensed Kase's gaze on me. We'd lock eyes until one of us would look away, until neither of us looked away. For the first time, I let myself believe that the latent attraction I felt for him for so long may not have been altogether one-sided. After a while, I stopped hearing what everyone else was saying. Wanting some time alone, I hiked up the falls until everyone's laughter was drowned out by the cascading water.

When I stopped long enough to look back, Kase was on my heels. The mist from the falls sparkled in the moonlight, floating between us, giving everything a dream-like quality. Then, for a few timeless moments, there was nothing between us but a kiss. A kiss that changed everything.

CHAPTER FIVE

"Miss June." Marty tips his hat as I pass through the front doors. "Going somewhere?"

"Um, yeah." I rest the heavy suitcase at my feet. I have no idea how to explain this unexpected trip to the McCasker farm, so I don't. "I'll be back in a couple weeks."

Just then a familiar white truck pulls up. Edwin kills the loud engine and steps out. He's really doing this. He yanks his suitcase out of the bed of the truck and climbs the steps toward me. Everything about him coming here to stay and me standing ready to leave seems surreal.

"Mr. McCasker." Marty moves forward but stops short, seemingly held fast by some invisible force.

Edwin grins and tosses him the keys. "Hey, Marty. You mind valeting the truck for me? Looks like I'm going to be staying a while."

Marty lifts his eyebrows. "Certainly, sir. I'm sorry. I didn't realize you were a guest." He rushes to take his bag and disappears into the hotel where the bellman waits, leaving us alone.

Edwin looks down at my suitcase. "Looks like you're ready to go."

I offer a tight smile. "Sure."

He meets my uncertain stare. "You okay with all this?"

"I've never stayed away from home this long before. I'm sure it'll be fine."

He rubs along the stubble on his jaw. "I just hope you're doing this for the right reasons, June. I'm not entirely sure Kase is."

My heart plummets south, landing like a stone in my stomach. "What do you mean?"

He sighs softly. "It's a complicated situation. I don't want you getting hurt."

In that instant, I'm not sure I know exactly why Kase is sending us all down this road. He's made his desire for me pretty clear, but under the electricity that crackles between us when we're close, I sense there's more behind this plan to bring me to the farm. I could guess all day, but only driving myself down the road to be with him will bring me the truth.

"Honestly, I'm not sure any of us are doing this for the right reasons," I say. After all, offering up my virginity to secure real estate hardly falls into the category of right. I must be insane, but it's too late to turn back now. "I can only hope that by the end of it, maybe we'll all understand each other better."

Edwin nods with a frown. "I hope for that too. I've spent half my life at odds with your father. I'm ready to forgive and forget."

Forgive and forget? What's to forgive?

"You and my mother were close," I say, reaching for the story the photo I found seemed to tell. My heart picks up speed at the knowing look in his eyes. "What really happened between you two?"

His frown deepens. "Not my story to tell, June." He takes his hat off and brushes over his hair. "Have a nice stay at the farm. Tell Kase to mind his manners." With a curt nod, he steps around me and disappears into the hotel.

I stand stunned for a moment before a sharp, cool wind makes me shiver in my sleeveless shirt and shorts. Dark clouds are rolling in on the other side of the valley. I walk quickly toward my Jeep in the lot. As I start the drive toward Kase, I wish we had a few more miles between us so I could think. But that's all I've done for years. Think. Wonder. Dream.

Maybe now was the time for acting, doing, and discovering the man Kase McCasker has become. He may get what he wants from me over the next two weeks, but damn it, so will I. I park in front of the farmhouse and climb the stairs with new determination.

I knock lightly on the screen door and peer into the quiet house before stepping inside. I drop my suitcase by the stairs. The cool valley breeze gusts through the hall, guiding me to the open back door. I step onto the back porch. Kase is on his knees just beyond, hands deep in the dirt, seemingly unaware of me. A basket filled with flower bulbs sits at his side.

"It's a little late for spring flowers, don't you think?" I lean forward on the railing and look down on him.

He looks up, his blue eyes bright and mesmerizing as always. "Hello to you too."

I smirk. "I knocked."

"Sorry. I'm not in the house much." He wipes his forehead and leans back on his haunches. "And, actually, I'm early with these. Supposed to plant the bulbs in the fall to root before the ground freezes. But I won't be here then. So, I'm getting them in the ground now." He stares thoughtfully down at the bed of dirt.

I hesitate, confused. "The house probably won't be here in the fall. Why are you bothering with flowers?"

He doesn't answer or meet my eyes. Instead he involves himself in the task of nesting more bulbs in the black dirt along the back side of the house. Content with the silence, I seat myself on the first step and watch him work. He seems lost in thought, his lips tight and his muscles rippling under his T-shirt with every deliberate motion. In this moment, I'm certain I could watch him work the land for hours on end and never tire of the view.

In the distance, the storm clouds catch on the top of the mountains. I wonder how long they'll linger there before covering the valley in shadows and rain. Could be an hour or a few. I bite my lip, uncertain what I'll do when the rain inevitably comes and traps us in the house together.

Rising to his feet, Kase tugs off his gloves and walks toward me. He tosses them on the steps, peels off his shirt, and wipes his face with it. The whole manual labor thing is definitely working in his favor. I clench my teeth to keep my jaw from sagging in awe. He's the same gorgeous, shirtless Kase I ran into days ago, and the effect on me is the same.

"So what do you want to see first?"

I lift my gaze from his perfect torso to his equally chiseled face. "Huh?"

He gestures to the horizon and the vast, sloping landscape of the McCasker land. "Of the property. I figured I could show you around a bit today."

"Oh." I laugh softly, but I can feel my cheeks heating.

"You didn't think I was going to ravage you the second you walked through the door, did you?"

I shake my head. "I have no idea what you're going to do one minute to the next, Kase."

He cracks a small smile. "I like it that way." He glances over his shoulder and back to me. "Come on. Looks like rain. We'll start with the house."

I ignore the jolt of anxiety in my belly and follow him inside to the kitchen.

He washes his hands and opens the fridge. "You hungry?"

It's past noon according to the clock on the wall, but my nerves must be obliterating my appetite, because all I can think about is Kase's next move.

"Not really," I say.

He straightens and shuts it, picking up an apple from the nearby fruit bowl. He sinks his teeth into it and leans casually against the counter. Jesus, how am I supposed to think straight when he looks this good eating produce?

"Do you normally walk around shirtless all day?"

He chuckles. "Is it a problem?"

"It's distracting." I fold my arms across my chest and avert my eyes.

"That's good to know," he says, setting the apple on the counter.

When he starts moving toward me, my gaze slides to his. His eyes are darker, his lids a little lower. I unfold my arms and step back unsteadily until the wall is behind me.

"What are you doing?" My voice is breathy.

He slows in front of me and props a hand on the wall. "Maybe we should just get this out of the way."

He's tall and imposing, threatening and tempting all at once. I inhale a shaky breath.

"You said..." I swallow hard. "You said you'd wait until I was ready."

Am I?

No. Definitely not.

Well, maybe a little.

He traps his lower lip between his teeth, dragging his hungry gaze up and down my body. "I did. But you've been here twenty minutes, and I haven't even touched you."

Then touch me already...

He answers my silent demand when he lowers his lips to mine. Just a brush. The softest touch. The hint of his taste with a rush of his scent, sweat and earth and something uniquely his. I don't wait for more. I lean in and claim the next sweep of our mouths. The kiss is slow and urgent at once, somewhere between asking and taking and savoring every second of contact. I slide my hands to his nape and bring our bodies closer.

Deliciously deep, our tongues dance and duel. All I can think is *more*. I need more...

"Kase," I whimper breathlessly. "Touch me... Please."

He kisses me again, angling so he can take my mouth deeper. The heat between us builds as we share breath. His hand travels down my body, settling on my hip.

"As soon as I get inside you, June, I'm never going to want to leave."

I love the sound of that. Endless hours, day after day tangled in Kase's sheets. I'm nearly writhing against him with the promise of it. I want him. I want all of it. Everything I've been yearning for all these years. And I want it now.

"I'm ready," I gasp, tearing our lips apart. "I'm ready now."

"You're not." He nips at my lower lip.

My desire morphs into something else—something needy and defensive. "How do you know I'm not ready?"

"For one, you're not begging me to fuck you."

Aren't I? I feel like I am, with every touch, every breathy moan that escapes me when we're touching this way. Is he really going to make me say it out loud?

"That's what you want? You want me to beg you when I've already promised you everything."

Something dark and mischievous glimmers in his eyes. "I can be a little demanding."

"I figured that out."

He's been nothing but bold and demanding since I walked back into his world.

He shakes his head slowly. "You have no idea what I'm capable of."

I close my eyes a moment, because something inside that threat makes me want to come apart on the spot. I'm convinced I could drown in his intense stares and dark promises right now and die a happy woman. "Why don't you show me?"

He tightens his grip on my hip. "You don't know what you're asking for."

"I'm still asking." Emboldened I begin to unbutton my poplin shirt. I don't know who this wanton woman inside me is, but I'm past caring.

His gaze drops to where my fingers work the buttons. "Are

you trying to seduce me, June?" His voice is dangerously low as his possessive touch falls away.

"Maybe." I release the last button, ready to peel the garment off and press our bodies together once more.

"Stop."

I freeze, paralyzed by his sharp tone. "Why? I thought—"

"Fold your arms behind you. Hands to your elbows."

I hesitate, even though I'm ready to crawl across the floor if it means getting him to touch me again. Reluctantly I do as he asks. The movement parts my shirt, revealing most of my white lace bra. The heat in my cheeks creeps down my chest. My heart and lungs are working overtime to keep up with the effect he has on me.

He trails his fingertip between my breasts and down my belly. "My God, June, you're beautiful. All you have to do is breathe and I want to rip your clothes off."

"Then do it," I beg. "What are you waiting for?"

"You're not ready for me yet."

"I am," I groan, pent-up frustration making every second without his hands on me nearly painful.

I need to feel him. I shift to move my arms, but he drops his hand from the wall, cinching my forearms together behind me in the space of a heartbeat. His hold is strong, as uncompromising as his tight expression.

He kicks my left leg out a few inches and tugs at the top button of my shorts. He dips his hand beneath the band, dragging his fingertips down the front of my panties. Lower and lower, until he finds his mark between my thighs where my clit throbs for his attention. Then he adds just enough pressure to make me cry out. My head falls back.

He brushes his lips along my jaw and whispers against my ear. "This is nothing. You know that, right? The things I'm going to do to you... I'm not going to hold anything back. We're going to shake the goddamn walls."

I'm speechless, enslaved by the promise. I barely stifle a groan as he ventures lower. He slides my panties to the side so I feel his flesh on mine.

He exhales roughly. "Jesus. When did you get wet for me?"

"Probably the minute I saw you."

He strokes me slowly, making me shiver every time he grazes my clit. I could come this way. I've done it a hundred times by myself, but somehow I know when Kase gives me an orgasm, it's going to turn me inside out like nothing ever has.

I roll my hips in time to his rhythm. He tightens his grip on my arms, and that reminder of his strength shoots a hit of something strong into my veins. My head is buzzing when he sinks his fingers lower...deeper.

He's barely penetrating me when he speaks again. "You're testing my patience, June." His tone is low, laced with lust and barely harnessed restraint.

I blink up at him, more than aware of the erection straining inside his jeans. "I wasn't aware you had any."

The muscles in his jaw flex, drawing my attention to the perfect lines there. Only one of the perfect, lickable lines of his body that I could spend hours studying...

"Before you started undressing in my kitchen, I did. But this..."

He sinks in a little deeper. I tense against him when I feel the sting of discomfort.

"This is why you'd better pray I have patience when I take you. Because right now the last thing I want to do is go slow. I want to fuck you against this wall and obliterate anything that comes between me and being as deep in you as I can get."

As much as I want that too, I get it. He's trying to make this good for me. The hint of pain is sobering, but not enough to make me want to stop where this is going.

Letting go of my arms, he withdraws, gently leaving my body. He takes a deep breath. As he does, I worry I'm losing ground.

"You don't have to go slow," I say, unable to hide the desperation in my voice. "I want this."

"How about lunch?"

He wraps his lips around his fingers, sucking my arousal from them. Even the wall may not be able to hold me up at the sight. Blood rushes to my arms where he held them so tightly. Every place he touched me still feels him, craves more of him. I'm little more than a ragdoll here, a puddle of unsatisfied need.

"Are you kidding me?"

He buttons my shirt up, one pale ivory button at a time. "I'm a shitty cook. And it's going to rain all afternoon. Let me take you out for a decent meal."

"You're really going to leave me this way?"

"Technically, I'm taking you with me this way." He sighs as he fastens the last button. "Trust me, I'm ready to crawl out of my skin right now. But I care about you enough to wait until I can do this right."

I shake my head, unwilling to accept this truth. "I thought that was up to me. That's what we agreed."

"It's a two-way street, beautiful." He leans in and kisses me gently. "Patience," he whispers.

And as he pulls away, putting unwelcome space between us, there's no question, I have absolutely none of that.

CHAPTER SIX

Kase pulls onto the main road that goes downtown. We're in his truck—which is only in slightly better condition than Edwin's old work truck—a steel blue with a matching interior leather seat.

For now, I'm grateful to be out of the house. Kase didn't give me the full tour, and I didn't ask for one, lest we get delayed in one of the bedrooms. I don't even know where I'm sleeping tonight, but if it's within two feet of him, I'm not sure how I'll survive.

"Where do you want to go?"

I think for a minute, mentally cataloging the sparse offerings downtown. "Mackie's, I guess."

Their pub fare is good. Maybe I'll catch Julie. Then again, I'm not thrilled with the way she preened like a peacock in front of Kase yesterday. Without a doubt, I'm staking my claim on Kase. At least until I know where this stint at the farmhouse will lead.

"It can get kind of crowded." Kase's focus stays on the road, his brows knit together.

"Late lunch on a Tuesday? I doubt it. Plus, there's no place else good to eat except the hotel. I'm guessing you don't want to go there."

He purses his lips. "Mackie's it is, then."

In a matter of minutes, we're pulling into the parking lot of Mackie's. We walk in together. Kase takes my hand as we weave through the tables in the barroom area. There's no sign of Julie, but I recognize her friend Priscilla behind the bar.

"Hey, Kase." She winks at him and heads toward us with menus.

Kase's grasp on my hand tightens. He turns to me as she approaches. "You sure you want to eat here?"

Before I can answer, she's right beside us. "Kase, what's up? You guys eating lunch?" She looks down at our clasped hands.

"We are," I say, drawing her attention back up.

"Great." She smiles tightly and gestures to a nearby table.

We take our seats. There are only a few things on the menu, so we give Priscilla our order, though her eyes rarely stray from Kase. When she leaves, the air is thick with a different kind of tension. I don't care for this kind as much.

"Do you know her?"

"Not especially well. Do you?" Kase raises an eyebrow, like he's challenging me.

"She's friends with Julie. I see her around from time to time." I strum my fingertips on the lacquered table. "She's really pretty," I add, throwing the challenge back to him.

Kase doesn't take the bait. Instead he clears his throat and leans in, resting his forearms on the small table.

"We have a lot to catch up on, June. I don't really want to talk about Priscilla. I want to talk about you."

He pins me with his blue-eyed stare. His hair falls in loose golden curls against his forehead and at the tops of his ears. A perfectly imperfect mess that I ache to run my fingers through.

I force myself to think about something else.

I'm tempted to press him about Priscilla. Why did she wink at him? Why did he want to leave the second he saw her? Why do all the women who work here seem to want to climb him like a tree?

Probably the same reason I do.

"Not much to talk about," I finally say. "This is Falls Edge, remember?"

"And people around here always have something to talk about."

Just then Priscilla brings our food. A burger for Kase and a French dip for me. I'm grateful when she doesn't linger.

I dig in, but Kase doesn't touch his food. "Tell me about the hotel."

I shrug. "The hotel is the way it's always been. People come and go. High season and low season. A celebrity stays with us every once in a while. That's the most excitement we see."

He takes a bite of his burger. "What about when you're not working at the hotel?"

"I take a few classes at the college every semester. Not a full course load, but enough to keep me busy between shifts."

He's quiet a moment. "Did you ever think about going away for school?"

"No. Wasn't really an option." I frown a little, because whenever people jet off for college and I'm left in this sleepy little town, I can't help but feel a twinge of resentment. I love Falls Edge, but sometimes my heart wants to wander too.

"Your dad has the money for it," he says.

"That's not it. If I really wanted to leave, he'd let me. I just know the hotel needs me. And I know that's where my future is. Seems pointless to leave only to come back to the same life, just four years older."

"Yeah," he mutters quietly. "I see what you mean."

I curse inwardly. "I didn't mean it that way."

"I knew what you meant, June. Trust me, every day I wake up here I wonder why I bothered trying to get away."

I chew in silence for a moment. I'm not unhappy he's back in Falls Edge, but he doesn't seem thrilled about the homecoming.

"Why did you come back, then? You could have used your degree somewhere else, I'm sure."

"I don't know. Something drew me back here. Maybe the farm." He polishes off the last of his burger and sits back in his seat. Something about his expression seems unsure, unsettled. "A purpose, I guess."

Something in my heart breaks. Because if taking over the farm was his purpose, this bargain will take that away. Instead of lingering on that note, I excuse myself to the ladies room. Priscilla comes out of one of the stalls as I enter.

"June."

"Hi," I say, slipping past her.

"So, tell me, are you two *together*?"

She says the last word like she can hardly believe it, let alone utter it.

I turn slowly to face her. "Something like that." I give her a forced smile, because however Kase and I choose to define these next two weeks is none of her business.

She crosses her arms and leans her hip against the sink. "I would have never guessed."

I lift my eyebrow. "Why is it so surprising that we would be together?"

Not many people outside our inner circle know about the rift between our fathers. Missing the chance to buy the land infuriated Daddy, but we'd kept the matter quiet in case Edwin ever changed his mind. Is it so unbelievable that Kase would want to be with someone like me?

She shrugs and turns toward the mirror, smoothing back her slick black hair. "He's kind of intense. Don't you think?"

I lock eyes with her reflection. "Kind of."

She turns back toward me, her face soft with concern. "Just be careful. I know we don't know each other well, but you're Julie's friend, so I feel like I should at least warn you."

I'd almost believe she was being sincere if I didn't get the strong feeling she wanted Kase for herself.

"Why would you need to warn me? I've known Kase most of my life."

Not well, granted. But outside of avoiding me for four years, he's never made me feel unsafe.

She lets out an exaggerated sigh and crosses her arms. "Listen. I didn't want to mention anything, but Kase and I hooked up a while ago. It was just... I don't know... Weird. I mean, he's extremely hot. Don't get me wrong. I'm just not into that scene. Like, if a guy wants to tie me up, I figure he's getting ready to hide a body."

She chuckles, and I force myself to join her. The truth is, I'm torn between scratching her eyes out and feigning concern to get more information out of her. I settle for a third option—pretending like I don't care and doing whatever I can to ward her off.

"Thanks, Priscilla. I appreciate your concern. I'm sorry it didn't work out between you two, but Kase and I definitely don't lack chemistry." I twist the end of my ponytail and shoot her a knowing smile that I pray sends her in the opposite direction.

The humor in her expression fades as she looks me up and down. She turns back toward the mirror and pinches her cheeks. "Whatever. Just thought you'd want to know what you're getting into," she mutters before disappearing out the door.

I exhale heavily, go into the stall, and mumble a string of curses to myself, though hurling them at Kase or Priscilla would be so much more satisfying. My mind is a chaotic jumble. Between this afternoon's almost-moment with Kase, Priscilla's warning about him, and knowing that, no matter what, in two weeks nothing will ever be the same between us, my thoughts don't know where to land.

When I return to the table a few minutes later, Kase is talking with an old buddy. His megawatt smile almost makes me forget how irritated I am.

"Hey, June." His blond friend is tall like Kase and built like a god. No wonder they're pals.

"Hey, Carter," I say, avoiding his eyes as I lift into my seat.

"How'd you manage to get Kase out of the house? We've been trying to get him out here for weeks."

Then I blurt out the first thing that pops into my head. "I promised he could tie me up later if we grabbed a bite to eat first."

Both men stare at me, slack-jawed. I shove a french fry into my mouth to silence any more unsavory comments from bursting free in the next thirty seconds or so.

"Wow. That sounds personal," Carter says with a laugh. He lifts his eyebrows and slaps Kase on the arm. "I guess I won't keep you. Good to see you, man."

"You too," Kase says, never taking his eyes off me.

When Carter disappears, Kase's expression hardens.

"I had a nice chat with Priscilla in the bathroom," I say.

"Let me guess. You launched a full-scale investigation into why she winked at me when we walked in."

"No, actually she ambushed me in there to warn me about your 'intensity.' Don't worry. I told her I was cool with all of it."

I eat a few more fries like we're not having one of the most awkward conversations of my life. Kase's stare burns hot like a brand on my skin.

"Are you?"

"I have no idea." I finally look up. "You know what I'm *not* cool with? Getting the lowdown from every girl in Falls Edge you've slept with."

"Thankfully it's a short list." His lips form a thin line.

"It's still a list." I toss my napkin on the table, get up, and head for the door.

"June. Wait."

I ignore him and leave the restaurant. The rain has started, but thankfully the truck is unlocked when I try the handle. I get in and try like hell to rationalize how I'm going to get through the rest of the night with Kase. Never mind the next two weeks.

He jumps into the truck a few minutes later, slamming the door loudly behind him. Maybe because it's an old truck. Maybe because he's mad. I don't give a damn.

"June—"

"Just take me home." I cross my arms tightly and try to peer through the rain streaming down the window. "*Your* home, I should say."

He cusses under his breath and starts the engine. We're heading out of town toward the farm as the rain hammers harder on the roof. It's more than a sprinkle. It's turned into a full-on deluge that causes Kase and the minimal traffic around us to slow.

"No one knows how to drive in the damn rain," he mutters. He swerves, passes a slowing car, and hits the gas to bring us back up to speed.

I grip the handle on the door. "Slow down."

He doesn't look at me. "I'm going five over. We're fine."

"No. You're going too fast."

"We're fine, June. It's just a little rain. Relax."

"If you want me to relax, slow down!" I suck in a panicked breath. My knuckles are white as I grip the handle. Sweat prickles against my palm on the seat.

He takes his foot off the gas. "Hey, I'm sorry." He reaches across and takes my hand. "We're slowing down, okay?"

I don't answer. Second by second, the panic ebbs away. My heartbeat returns to normal. Then he turns onto a side road that I know won't take us home.

CHAPTER SEVEN

"We're just going to park for a few minutes until this rain stops."

Kase pulls the truck into an empty lot at the head of one of the many hiking trails. There's nothing but trees and gravel around us. Nothing but the sound of the rain falling in heavy sheets and the hum of the engine.

I'm grateful for a minute to collect myself, even though I'm certain he must think I'm crazy. Between my earlier comments and now my weather anxiety, he's likely wondering why he invited a lunatic into his life.

"I'm sorry," I finally say. "My mom died in a car accident."

He squeezes my hand gently. "I know."

I press my eyes closed. "When the weather's bad, I can't help but think about it when I'm on the road. I'm sorry I yelled at you."

"I'm sure I more than deserved it."

I laugh softly. "You did. Just not for that." I shake my head. "I guess it's starting to make sense why I never left Falls Edge. I can't even handle a little rain. You must think I'm—"

"You're human. And you don't entirely trust me yet. It's fine. We all have our hang-ups."

I draw my free hand into my lap. "What are yours, Kase?"

He pauses. "I don't know. I guess I have a few."

"Priscilla seems to think so." I pray he doesn't hate me for bringing this up, but I have to know more.

He sighs. "Gotta love small towns."

"Why did she tell me to be careful of you?"

He stares blankly ahead. "Because when she's not sneaking shots behind the bar, she's spreading mindless gossip."

"What happened between you?"

"We're not talking about this."

I rip my hand out of his grasp. "Yes, we are."

"Damn it, June." He shoves his hands through his damp hair. "Let's just say we weren't compatible. We both had a few too many at Mackie's one night and ended up at her place. We started messing around, I misread the signals, and realized too late that she didn't enjoy my flavor of kink. I don't think it traumatized her too much, though, because she hasn't stopped texting me wanting round two since I got back into town."

My jaw falls but I snap it back shut. I'm still upset with both of them. Priscilla just slid into first place, but knowing that Kase took her to bed has me feeling suddenly sick.

"You left Falls Edge making me believe you cared about me. Hell, you told me you cared about me today. How am I supposed to believe any of it when you came home and slept with someone like her?"

"June, you have no idea what you're talking about. Not a goddamn clue. Let's just go home."

He reaches for the gear shift, but I stop him, taking his hand in mine again.

"Tell me why I wasn't good enough. Just tell me."

"You were too good, okay?" The intensity burning behind his eyes steals my next breath. "And for the record, I didn't sleep with Priscilla that night. We didn't get that far. But if she hadn't wigged out I would have, because I was at a point in my life where I didn't give a damn about anything. Wasting the night with her would have been just the thing to make me forget about shit I didn't want to think about. For four years, I chased every impulse and fed every fucked-up desire. I poured gasoline on a mountain of pain you'll never understand and gambled on there being something worth living for in the ashes."

I caress my fingertips against his, silently hoping he knows that under all the frustration and my own hurt, I care. Even if I don't understand who or what could have hurt him so badly.

"I wasn't going to bring you into that mess, June," he says, his tone softer. "And if I'd even considered it, your father would have cut it off before we ever began. You know that as well as I do."

I bite the inside of my cheek. He's not wrong. Daddy was never especially strict with me growing up. I had more freedom than most. But when it came to the McCaskers, he would have made a relationship with Kase damn near impossible.

Things are different now though. I'm a grown woman.

I slide closer, reach up to touch his face, and guide his attention back to me, away from whatever troubled memories have darkened his thoughts.

"What changed? Why now?"

He looks into my eyes before lowering his gaze to my mouth. He leans in and brushes his lips sweetly against mine. "I found you in the ashes," he whispers against me.

My heart beats fast against my ribs. I don't speak. I answer with a kiss filled with all the things I'm not sure how to say. All the nights I'd wanted him. All the affection that grew around his absence. And now a piece of my heart wants to mend the pain in his. He circles his arm around me, bringing our torsos flush. With that single act, I feel us launched back to where we were in the kitchen hours ago. So lost in the moment that we could barely stop ourselves.

"Kase... You can't wind me up and leave me hanging like that again. I can't take it."

He answers by lifting me so I'm straddling him, my bare calves resting on the outsides of his thighs. "How about I don't leave you hanging this time?"

In that instant, I don't care that we're in the cab of his truck. I just need to feel him. Need to show him with my body what I can't tell him with words. I sift my fingers through his hair and bring our mouths together. As we kiss, he feverishly works the buttons on my shirt and pushes it over my shoulders. My bra is loosened a second later. When he breaks the kiss, the lacy garment falls away and my breasts fall gently against my chest.

The air seems supercharged. Anticipation. Heat. Desire so potent it's almost painful, saturating the space between us and all around us. My skin is pebbled with goosebumps. My nipples ache to be touched. I swivel my hips in his lap, needing to know that he's affected too. Without a doubt, he is.

Before I can touch him there, he pushes me back and grazes his palms up my sides until they're covering my breasts. I arch into his touch, needing more than a gentle caress.

"You're perfect." The raw appreciation in his voice reaches

deeper than his words.

I bite my lip and shift my hips again, a frustrated moan crawling up my throat. He grasps my breasts and brings his mouth to them, one by one, flicking his tongue against the hardened tips before sucking hard and peppering the skin around each nipple with tiny bites.

I hold him against me, fisting my hands in his hair. He feasts on my breasts for what seems like forever, until my skin is dark pink and raw from his tongue and teeth. The mild pain is like a scratch on the itch of my desire, only heightening my need for more. I'm past wound up. Past modesty and good reason. Before I can beg him to take the rest of me, he flips me so my back hits the seat.

His lips are parted, his breathing as ragged as mine, as he unbuttons my shorts and drags them down my thighs, taking my panties with them.

Only then does panic hit me. I'm stark naked. In Kase's truck. Only the persistent rain and the condensation building up on the windows from the heat of our bodies gives us privacy from anyone who would happen upon us. I reach to cover myself, but Kase grabs my wrists and lifts my hands away.

"Too late for modesty, June." He takes my foot and guides it to his other side so his body takes the space between my legs.

Heat rushes to my cheeks and radiates down every limb at being so exposed. "What if someone catches us out here?"

He lowers his head and sinks his teeth into the inside of my thigh. I jerk and try to draw my thighs closer, but he holds me open, his grasp firm. "Not sure I'll care. I've waited too long to taste you."

He continues his assault on my flesh, licking and nibbling up my thighs until he's got nowhere else to go.

"Kase..."

He hushes me. But the second his tongue hits my clit, I suck in a sharp breath. I push his shoulder and try to scoot away. He catches my wrist and yanks my hips down so my sex is an inch from his lips.

"Where do you think you're going?" His eyes are dark, molten with lust.

"Nowhere. I'm just... I don't know. I'm nervous. No one's ever done that."

"I'm glad. But you'd better wrap your head around it quick because we're not leaving here until I hear you screaming my name." He rotates my wrist and plants a kiss on my palm. "And if you don't learn how to control your hands, I'm going to find a way to tie them up."

Good God.

He drags his fingertips up and down my slit, parting my folds and blowing a puff of air on my sensitive flesh. I nearly cry out again. I clench my hands into fists.

When he licks me again, his gaze fixes on mine, a tractor beam of intimacy. "Does that scare you?"

I shake my head. Hell if it doesn't turn me on even more.

"Good," he murmurs, his breath tantalizing my skin there.

The sensation compounds with the others. His lips, his fingers, his tongue. Heaven help me, his tongue. I lift my arm and curl my fingers around the door handle. My eyes roll back, and I lift my hips against his mouth. This has to be what heaven feels like. Pure surrender.

My body climbs, like a taut wire coiling deep inside me, one perfect turn after the next. When his teeth nudge where his tongue and fingertips have teased me to a near breaking point, I cry out loudly and jolt hard.

I can't hold back anymore. I let my hand tangle in his golden locks.

"That's it, beautiful. Hold on," he rasps against my flesh.

When his finger slips inside me with less care than before, the sudden pang shocks me momentarily out of my blissful climb.

My eyes flash open and lock with his. "What are you doing?"

"You're going to let me make love to you, right?"

I blink. "Yes."

He twists inside me gently. The sensation isn't unpleasant.

"Okay, then I'm getting us halfway there. Just relax and let me make you feel good."

"But..."

Ignoring me, he resumes, licking me enough to scatter my thoughts again.

"June, I would never hurt you."

With heavy-lidded eyes, I drag my fingertips across his scalp. "I trust you."

With that, he closes his eyes and latches on to me with more pressure and mind-bending teeth-tongue combination moves that have me *this* close to screaming his name in rapture. Every shallow dive inside my tight channel makes me want more of him there, all of him, as deep as he can go. I need to make him feel as incredible as he's making me feel right now. He adds another finger to his efforts. I'm too close to coming to care about the pain that knocks a little harder with each stroke.

"God. Oh God... Kase..."

"That's it, baby. You're going to come for me."

"Stop talking, Kase. Just... Ah!"

I scream when he clamps his teeth around my clit and lashes his tongue against me unmercifully. My hips buck wildly until he pins them down firmly with his forearm. I'm right on the edge. Barely breathing. Clawing at the door and the leather. Tugging at the beautiful head between my thighs. Then everything tilts.

I drag in a ragged breath only to have Kase's name tear from my lips with a feral groan. Like a sweeping wildfire, the orgasm rips through me and consumes everything. Every layer of my being. From my scorching skin to my tortured core as his fingers plunge deeper. Past the sharp stab of pain and straight into the deep, drowning pleasure that's owning me, bringing every fantasy I'd ever entertained about this moment to life in the most satisfying way possible.

I'm pretty sure even the sweat clinging to me is currently residing in a state of weightless bliss when Kase slips out of me. I'm barely conscious when he pulls my panties and shorts on. I open my eyes and he takes my hand, lifting me to a seated position beside him.

His eyes glitter with warmth, and his glistening smile is the definition of smug. When he pulls me in for a kiss, I moan into him. He's warm velvet. My arousal lingers on his tongue. He caresses every inch of my exposed skin as if he can't stop. Hell, I don't ever want him to stop. Never going to leave this cloud. Never leaving Kase. Never leaving this damn truck...

"Woohoo!"

We break away and look out the front window. The rain has

stopped, and the condensation is sparse enough in one spot to clear our view of two teenagers at the head of the trail, pointing and laughing. No doubt about it. We've been caught.

"Shit!" I scramble for my clothes.

My bra is somewhere on Kase's side, but my shirt is crumpled on the floor near my feet. As soon as I get my hands on it, Kase throws the truck into reverse and tears out of the lot.

CHAPTER EIGHT

I turn in bed with a stretch. The morning air is cool on my skin, and the faint sounds of farm equipment float in through the cracked window. I open my eyes and squint against the early morning sunlight filling the bedroom.

The events of yesterday come back to me as I blink awake. The mortifying experience of being caught making out half naked in Kase's truck shoots to the forefront of my thoughts. I groan and turn my face into the pillow.

I wish I could bring myself to regret it. I really should. I'm twenty years old and really should know better than to be so reckless. But Kase's hands on me—sweet merciful God, his mouth on me— was like nothing I'd ever experienced. I'm not sure I would take the moment back if half of Falls Edge happened upon us.

Luckily, they hadn't, and as we sped off for home, I could barely get my shirt back on before succumbing to an uncontrollable fit of laughter. Hard as I tried, I couldn't stop, a circumstance that proved contagious when Kase lost his composure too.

Once we caught our breath back at the farmhouse, I'd half expected Kase to have his wicked way with me. He certainly could have. Even though I was sated, my body still hummed from the incredible orgasm he'd pulled from me. Still, in the hours after, he exercised restraint he didn't have before. We spent the evening in front of the television, curled up together, talking sometimes, kissing other times. Always touching but never going further.

When I was too sleepy to keep my eyes open, he helped me get settled in the guest room for the night. I didn't ask why he wasn't inviting me into his bed, but a little part of me appreciated the space. As much as I wanted to stay close to him, I wasn't quite sure what it would be like to sleep next to someone in a strange bed and strange house.

More awake now, I sit up and look around the room. This isn't home. But it's *a* home. A house. A little thrill runs through me with that thought.

Wallpaper with yellow roses covers the bedroom walls. The antique furniture is minimal—a small bureau and an end table by my bed. The quilt covering my legs is a patchwork of floral pastels, softened by age. How long has it lived in this house? I get the feeling much of what fills the McCasker farmhouse has been here through several generations of his family.

Eager to explore more and find Kase, I shower and dress quickly. With bare feet, I descend the stairs and take a short tour through the empty first floor. Kase must be working. The note he leaves in the kitchen confirms it.

June, future queen of the McCasker farm...

Hope you slept well. I'll be in the pasture all day. Make yourself at home. I'll be back before sundown.

Kase

P.S. Didn't sleep a wink last night thinking of you.

I smile. Butterflies flit around my belly. Warmth floods me the same way it does when Kase is near. Immediately I regret that I have to spend the day without him. Still, Kase neglecting the garden isn't quite the same as neglecting the farm. The livestock needs attention regardless of the property's fate.

I poke around the kitchen, finding its amenities sparse. The fridge is nearly bare. The cupboards are stocked with canned food and an economy-sized pack of instant macaroni and cheese—Kase's specialty and our dinner last night. I'm used to relying mostly on the hotel's kitchen for sustenance. I'm not sure I can survive on what's here.

Opening the last cupboard, I find a stack of old cookbooks. Their covers are yellowed, but I flip through the first one titled *Miss Dixie's Home Cooking*. I take a mental note of a few promising dishes and step away to pour myself a cup of coffee from the brewed pot on the counter.

I scoop up the rest of the cookbooks, move to the dining room, and take a seat at the head of the large farmhouse table that fills almost the entire room. I set aside Miss Dixie's culinary wisdom. The next one has a simple cover with a sketch of a cornucopia. I open the first page, and in thick pencil strokes it reads Haidee's Recipes.

Inside are pages filled with dozens of handwritten recipes. The more I read, the hungrier I get. I'm strangely motivated too. I'm certain my cooking prowess is no better than Kase's, but seeing the handwritten recipes inspires something in me. Maybe being here makes me want to play house, because I've never actually had one to myself that I didn't have to share with hundreds of guests and hotel staff. Plus, when's the last time Kase enjoyed a home-cooked meal?

With nothing else on the agenda except to wait for Kase to finish work, I grab my keys and head to the store to stock the kitchen for the week. I'm not sure either of us can stomach any more meals out at Mackie's.

I spend the afternoon shopping and then claiming the first floor as my domain. I discover silver flatware and placemats from the sideboard in the dining room. To complete the setting for dinner, I pluck a few lilies from the front path and place them in a white ceramic glass vase for the dining room table. The smallest touches make the house seem a little brighter and less like the sparse bachelor pad that Edwin and Kase have been content with.

Moving on to the kitchen, I organize the food I picked up shopping and map out a plan for dinner. Country fried chicken, creamed corn, and homemade biscuits are on the menu. Ambitious? Maybe. Never mind that I've barely cooked a scrambled egg for myself without the help of one of the hotel's chefs. The new space and seemingly endless stretch of time is too inviting to pass up though.

As the sun sinks toward the horizon, I buzz around the kitchen, moving from bowls of flour and egg batter to the cast iron frying pan I could barely lift onto the burner. I drop in some breaded chicken breasts and jerk back when the hot oil crackles and pops toward me.

When boots drop on the back porch, I hurry to investigate. I smile as Kase comes into view. I push open the screen door and lean against the jamb. "Welcome home."

His face is flushed, and his clothes are covered in a thousand little green specks of grass like he's been mowing all day.

"You look like you've been up to something." He looks me up and down with that subtle hunger in his eyes that does something to my insides every damn time.

I glance down at my clothes. My cutoffs and T-shirt are covered in flour and various stains from my cooking adventures. I reach for my hair, tucking one of many loosened strands back into my messy bun. God, I must look like a hot mess. Probably not the sexy house guest he was looking forward to seeing.

Before I can make excuses, he frowns and sniffs the air. "Is something burning?"

My eyes go wide. "Oh no!" I turn on my heel and run to the kitchen.

Smoke is billowing off the frying pan. Panicked, I swish my hands in the air above it. Suddenly Kase is beside me, his hand on the burner knob.

"You've got the heat a little high, babe." He lowers the flame singeing the chicken in the pan. "There. That's better."

"I'm sorry—"

"It's fine now. Here." He plucks the tongs from the counter and flips the chicken, revealing the charred black side.

As the smoke dissipates, I sigh with some relief and no small amount of embarrassment. After a whole day's planning, I still burned our dinner to a blackened crisp. Fabulous.

"You okay?"

I look up at Kase, trying to blink away the tears stinging my eyes.

"What's wrong, baby? Don't be upset."

His sweet words make the emotions well up even harder. Am I crying over chicken? I shrug and wipe at my eyes. "I wanted to do something nice for you."

He laughs softly, but his expression smooths again as he cups my cheeks, forcing me to meet his gaze. His eyes glitter with warmth and something else—something I can't name.

"Thank you," he says softly. He bends so our faces are close and kisses the tip of my nose. "This is the nicest thing anyone's done for me in a long time. You really didn't have to cook for me."

I swallow over the knot in my throat. Before I can explain about the recipe book and everything else, he leans in and kisses away all my thoughts. I don't know how long we stand that way, tasting each other like the day kept us apart too long. He smells like grass and sweat, and I can't get enough of him. I lean in so more of our bodies touch. Then a pop from the stove startles me.

"Damn it," he says. "Now *I'm* burning our dinner." He nudges me back and deftly moves the well-done chicken from the pan onto a plate.

I sulk a little. Dinner is a long way from being what I'd hoped for. Thankfully I battered enough chicken to attempt another batch. I'm about to get started on that when the egg timer starts dinging.

"Oh no! Crap, crap, crap. I totally forgot."

I grab two towels and push Kase out of the way so I can open the oven. I pull out the tray of biscuits that I hadn't bothered to check on. Then a little bubble of happiness comes to the surface as I rest them on the unoccupied burners and survey the results.

"I can't believe it. I can't believe I didn't screw these up." The biscuits are nicely formed and only a little browned. Haidee's recipes didn't have pictures, but these are exactly how I imagined they should turn out.

"There you go," Kase says. "This is your specialty. Biscuits. They are utterly perfect." He lightly taps the top of one.

"We'll see how they taste, I guess."

"I'm sure they're amazing. Ow." He jerks his hand back after trying to pull one loose. "I will gladly be the guinea pig the minute they cool off. Let me go clean up, and I'll be right down." He kisses me swiftly on the lips and disappears up the stairs.

I take a deep breath, restored enough to try salvaging my somewhat botched meal. Thankfully, I have better luck with the second round of chicken without distractions.

Kase's timing is perfect. He comes behind me and wraps his arms around my waist as I plate up two dishes. He's warm and damp from his shower. When he kisses my neck, I almost spoon the corn onto the floor.

"Quit it, Kase. I'm trying to feed us, for heaven's sake."

"Sorry. You're just so very sexy when you're being domestic."

"Don't get too used to it. This clearly isn't my calling."

He releases me with a chuckle, and we take our plates to the dining room.

"Wait for me next time," he says. "We can figure out dinner together."

"You're the reason I burned it to begin with. You're too distracting." I'm only half kidding. I can't imagine concentrating on much of anything when he's around. He has the unique ability to make me forget what I'm doing in the space of a look.

I set my plate at the head of the table where I'd planned my culinary masterpiece earlier. Then I halt.

"Sorry. Is this your spot?"

Kase frowns, confused. "For what?"

"For meals."

He laughs. "June, my spot is in front of a TV tray in the living room. Takes my mind off the taste of powdered cheese and loneliness. So, please. Sit. You've earned that spot with our feast."

I offer a hesitant smile and lower into the seat. We eat in silence for a few minutes. The chicken is decent. Corn and creamy butter is reliably tasty. And the biscuits... I take a bite into one just as Kase does. I study his face as I chew on the fluffy goodness.

His eyes close with a moan. "Oh yeah. Biscuits are definitely your thing."

I smile broadly, proud that I did at least one recipe in the book justice. "It's okay for a first try, I suppose. I found some old cookbooks in the cupboard. Who's Haidee? This was her recipe."

"That's my grandmother. She and my grandfather passed away before I was born. Edwin had already taken over the farm."

I take another bite of my biscuit. My thoughts hover around the obvious void, the space where his mother should be.

"Where is your mom?"

He keeps his attention on his meal. "She ran off when I was little. She wasn't ready to be a mom, I guess. Edwin raised me."

"I'm sorry," I say quietly. I'd like to know more but sense that I'm hedging a sensitive subject. I've spent all day waiting to be with him again, so I decide to keep the mood light. "At the risk of sounding totally cliché, how was your day?"

He chews his bite, a small smile creeping in. "Better than most, I suppose, because I had seeing you to look forward to."

"Do you like the work you do here?"

He shrugs. "It's all right. I don't dislike it. I didn't have a plan after graduation, so when I came back, I realized how much needed to be done around here. Even with a couple guys helping us out here and there, it's a lot to keep up between Edwin and me."

I push the corn around my plate, hoping to avoid acknowledging that this job and the responsibilities that go with maintaining the property will be disappearing before long.

"How about you? How was your day? I see you're putting your mark on our bachelor pad." He nods toward the vase of tiger lilies.

"I hope you don't mind. They were blooming, so I thought we could enjoy them inside."

He traces his fingertip under a curled petal. "Edwin always said they were my mom's favorite. I guess when someone's been missing from your life for so long, you don't have much else to cling to but little things like that."

My heart aches for him all over again. I can relate to being motherless, but knowing that my mother was taken from me too soon has to be different than feeling purposefully abandoned. I don't know how to ease that pain for him, but something inside me wants to make him feel less alone with it.

"I missed you today," I say softly.

He looks over, as if my words pulled him away from another place. "Did you now?"

"Don't let it go to your head," I say quickly, even though I don't mean it.

"It already has, believe me." His crooked smile makes me want to kiss it off him. "But I'm thinking it has everything to do with me leaving you in this old house by yourself all day."

I shrug. "I didn't mind so much. It's so different from what I'm used to. I mean, the hotel is beautiful. But this..."

I tug my lower lip between my teeth. How do I explain to him how simply being in a home can inspire such potent feelings? I'm not sure how to share the sentiment without acknowledging the inevitable demise of the house. Unfortunately, avoiding the minefield of that topic is becoming increasingly difficult the more time I spend around Kase.

"I'm enjoying being here more than I expected to," I finally say.

CHAPTER NINE

As dusk sinks over the valley, I sit, legs tucked against my chest, on the back-porch swing. For a moment, I wonder how Daddy is getting by without me at the hotel. The thought is swiftly overwhelmed when I think of Kase. I can't say there's anywhere else I'd rather be right now. Not even home.

After dinner, Kase had ordered me out here to relax while he finished cleaning up. Somehow, I already miss him. His touch. His attention. The way I feel like the most important person in his world. As long as we're here this way, together, existing in this little bubble that our arrangement created, he's becoming the most important person in mine too.

Ten minutes later, Kase joins me. He leans on the peeling whitewashed railing, legs crossed casually at the ankle. "Thanks again for dinner. It was delicious."

I give him a small smile. "I'm glad you liked it."

He stares down at me. His gaze seems to penetrate my skin, touching every part of me, from my messy hair to my bare toes.

That quickly, I get the sense that I'm being hunted. That Kase is making plans for us—for *me*—somewhere in the depths of his mind. It knots me up inside.

"What are you thinking about?"

He turns and looks out at the mountains, which are now saturated in deep reds and oranges. "The answer to that question is always you, June." He glances back at me, a new rigidity to his posture. "The longer we wait, the harder it's going to be for me to do this right."

The air presses out of my chest with his confession. I'd be lying if I said I hadn't devoted every other minute of today wondering if we'd go further tonight. If he'd finally take me the way I've been damn near begging him to.

"I told you I was ready."

He curls his fingers over the edge of the railing. "You think you are because you have no idea what's in my head right now."

I wait patiently for him to tell me.

He strums his fingers on the rail, looking down. "You know what I did last night?"

I shake my head.

"I imagined all the filthy things I wanted to do to you. It was a nonstop erotic slideshow that I couldn't shut off no matter how hard I tried. All goddamn night I had to convince myself not to go into your room and make every one of those fantasies come true."

"What do you want to do to me?" My whisper lingers in the air between us. An invitation that draws him closer, one slow, confident step in front of the other, until he's settled on his haunches in front of me.

He cups my ankles and tugs until my feet hit the floor. Never breaking eye contact, he spreads my legs wider, sliding his palms along the sensitive insides of my thighs. "Tease you. Make you want me as badly as I want you."

I close my eyes at the recollection of his fingers plunging inside me yesterday, awakening sensations I'd never known before. He must have no idea how badly I want him already.

His gliding touch up each of my arms draws my attention away from the memory and back to the living, breathing Kase. "Slowly..." He digs his thumbs into the crease of my elbows and drags slowly down. "Methodically...until every cell of your beautiful body cries out for more."

I suck in a breath, acutely aware of how the rough trail of his nails down my skin feeds the fire raging in my core.

"I want to turn you on until it hurts. Then I want to press into that hurt and find out how far you can go, how much you can take until you break."

My heart races. My blood sings, hot and needy through my veins. "You... You want to break me?" I swallow, but my throat is dry.

"I do." He lowers to kiss my wrists and licks up the faint red line he drew up my forearm. "I want to dominate you. Control you. Push you. Fuck you."

A shiver works its way through my whole body. I'm suddenly too warm. My nipples are tight, needy beads under my shirt. The arousal between my legs is tied to every dirty word that spills from his perfect lips. I squirm, jutting my hips another inch toward him.

"Do what you want, Kase. I told you already. I trust you."

He stares at me a moment. His body totally still. His gaze seems to search for a reason not to believe my words match my intent.

Kase is different. Intense beyond words. And from what I already know about him, he's a doorway to the kind of pleasure I've only dreamt about.

He threads our fingers together.

"Nothing about this arrangement between us—the property or your time here—means you're obligated to do things with me that you're not comfortable with. You can tell me to stop. I'll do everything in my power to make sure you're more than satisfied. But if it's ever more than you can handle, all you have to do is say so."

I'm ready to say yes to anything. All of it. I'll sign in blood if I have to. Sure, I'm afraid of what I don't know yet about Kase and his dark promises, but that fear lives inside an intimate kind of trust that grows between us day by day. I've never felt such a contradiction like this with another human being in my life, but it feels so damn right.

"Where do we start?" The question is breathy, laced with invitation.

He doesn't budge. "Say you understand. I need to know your limits, and I can't know unless you're willing to tell me."

I lean forward. Our noses touch... Our lips nearly do. "Kase." I draw my palm across his rough cheek and my thumb along his lower lip. "No one's ever made me feel the way you do. Before you ever touched me, I wanted you to. Nothing's changed except I know you better, and I want you so much more. So put your hands on me. Dominate me." I hover my lips above his and flick my tongue against his mouth. "Fuck me."

With a growl, he consumes the space between us, sealing our mouths in a savage kiss. His arms come around me, and in a flash, I'm wrapped around him. He moves us out of the night air, into the house, and up the narrow stairs. Our lips never stop seeking. I touch him everywhere I can reach. I tug at his soft white T-shirt as we pass into his bedroom and fall onto the bed. He tears my hand from the hem and pushes it and the other into the mattress above my head, pinning me.

Kneeing my legs apart, he settles between them. I can feel my heartbeat through my whole body. In my swollen lips when our kisses get deeper and more desperate. At my wrists where he holds me tightly. All my senses are on high alert. His jeans are rough against my thighs. Every grind of his hips teases what's to come. The weight and strength of his body matches the dominating hold he has on me. It's comforting and arousing all at once.

But my skin prickles for more... More contact, more skin on skin.

He trails his touch over my belly and under my shirt. Dipping under my bra, he traps my nipple between his fingertips and pinches until I whimper.

I wriggle in his grasp, which only tightens when I resist. "Let me touch you," I beg.

His eyelids lower a fraction. "No. I like it this way." His gaze roves over me hungrily. "I think I'm harder than I've ever been in my life, seeing you pinned like this, just waiting to find out how I'm going to fuck you. It's taking all my willpower not to tie you to the goddamn bed right now. I could tease you for hours."

I exhale a shaky breath as I try to process all of that. I've been so on edge for days. I'm not sure how I can survive hours more of this craving.

"Please..."

"Please, what, baby?" He grinds against me, eliciting a whole-body shudder.

"Kase," I mewl, turning my head to the side.

"Look at me when you beg. Or I'll put you on your knees and show you what real begging feels like."

I whip my gaze to his. My cheeks heat and my next few breaths come quickly with his threat. The dark look in his eyes tells me not to challenge it. The idea of getting on my knees for him isn't wholly uncomfortable. Being there doesn't get him any closer to being inside me, though. So I give him what I think he wants.

"I thought about you all day. The same way you thought about me last night. Kase, I fantasized about this night a thousand times." I swallow, because a part of me hates being this vulnerable. But he has to know it...

He reaches for my shorts, tugs on the top button, and drags the zipper down slowly. "What did you fantasize about?"

"Us at the falls that night. Sneaking back to the hotel, going to my room."

He slides his hand down and teases his fingertips over my panties, derailing my thoughts. "How did I touch you?"

I bite my lip and try not to moan. "Like this. Just like this."

"Then what?"

"You undressed me."

Slowly he releases my wrists and, pushing my shirt up, places a hot kiss against my belly that makes me quiver. Hooking his fingers under the band of my shorts, he pulls them down with my panties.

"And how did that make you feel, being so naked and exposed in your fantasy?" He stands by the bed and pulls his shirt off.

I try to formulate words, but everything gets muddled when he shucks his pants and stands before me. A tower of muscle and mouthwatering desire. As if my focus isn't already riveted on his thick cock jutting out from his muscled body, he strokes it leisurely, and I'm fixated. My pulse thrums a heavy, steady beat that I can feel between my thighs.

He opens a drawer in the bedside table and pulls out a condom.

"I asked you a question, June. How did it feel?"

He brings it to his teeth and tears the wrapper before slowly rolling it onto his considerable length.

"Scary," I say, my voice shaky and breathy. "Intimate. Like this."

He comes toward me, and I think I might combust when he tears my shirt and bra off, bringing our bodies together, hot and flush. When he kisses me, I feel his teeth and his waning restraint.

"Then what?" His voice is like gravel, vibrating through me.

"You... You..." I shake my head. Not being able to form the words suddenly makes me feel like the shy sixteen-year-old girl whose desire Kase lit on fire all those years ago.

He notches the head of his cock against my opening, and my breath catches.

"I fantasized about you too," he whispers. "About this." Then he pushes in, meeting that tender spot his fingers found back in his truck. He lingers there, pinning me with his stare. Those two blue oceans ease me into the piercing pain that comes with the surge of his body joining completely with mine.

A small cry escapes my lips, and I cling to him. He's the force behind the discomfort, but somehow he's my salvation too.

"You were always the one," he says softly.

I blink through the haze of my pain and the rush of the moment.

"This is always where I wanted to be. I knew I could never have you, but I never forgot about you, June. Never stopped wishing that night had ended the way you envisioned."

I wrap my legs around his waist and hold him to me. "You have me now."

CHAPTER TEN

He bands his arm around my hips and seats himself deeper, causing me to suck in a sharp breath. But the look in his eyes seems to reach deeper still. Dark-blue tornados of lust. His lips part as he pulls back and sinks in again, stealing my breath with the perfectly overwhelming way he fills me.

Emotion seizes my throat. It's as if the second I let him inside me, everything changed. Our bodies fused and the chemicals in my brain rewired. Now all I can see is his face, gorgeous and vulnerable, as he slowly begins making love to me. All I can feel is this electric frenzy that drives his thrusts and my gnawing hunger for more of them. All I can think about is how perfectly we fit. How perfect this could always be...

I let my whirling thoughts run wild and lose myself in another velvet kiss. Kase's thrusts are agonizingly slow. He makes me feel every inch of him, every tender drag against where he's torn through my virginity, every dizzying blow when he reaches the deepest part of me.

I fit my heels into the indentations of his taut ass and add pressure to his next thrust. I feel possessed, crazed with how badly I want to be consumed by this man. "Kase, I need more."

His muscles tense, but he keeps his pace. "I don't want to hurt you."

I dig my fingernails into his shoulder and arch into him. "Yes, you do."

A low moan rumbles through him. "June... Not tonight."

"I've waited this long. Make me feel all of it."

"Fuck," he breathes against my neck. Then he glances between us where he withdraws slowly to the tip. "God help me, I want to hurt you in all the best ways."

I spread my legs infinitesimally more, as if somehow I can bring him into me again by sheer will. The yellow lamp on the bedside table casts shadows on us, darkening his eyes behind the short curtain of his wavy locks, bringing every ridge of his abdomen and defined muscles into stark relief. He's beautiful and intense and so much more than I ever imagined he could be. And right now, tonight, we belong only to each other.

"Are you sure that's what you want?"

Another heat wave starts in my cheeks and warms me down every limb. Why does the idea of unleashing the beast in him make me melt this way?

Who the hell am I?

"Don't hold back," I whisper.

He slips out of me completely and starts moving down my body. I make a small sound of protest. I claw at his shoulders to draw him back to me, but he's too powerful and too fast. He brings his mouth down on my pussy before I can argue. Maneuvering his tongue and teeth and fingers, he teases and taunts until I'm grinding against every touch.

I writhe and whimper. His mouth is magic. *Kase* is magic...

"You want to come?"

"Yes," I moan, tugging his hair, desperate for the last few strokes that'll push me over the edge. I'm so close. So incredibly close...

"Not yet."

I let out a small scream when he unlatches from pleasing me and slides up my body again.

"What are you doing to me?" I can't hide my desperate tone. I need him to finish me. I need...*something.*

He grabs my thigh, pushes it to my chest, and lines his cock up to me again. "Getting you ready."

"For what?"

"For this," he says the same moment he slams into me.

I cry out when every inch of him fills me at once. He withdraws quickly and slams home again.

I grab his arms and stare up at him, trembling. His gaze never wavers. His body is a column of raw determination.

He powers into me without restraint. It borders on painful. It's exactly what I asked for, but it awakens something new. A kind of pleasure that nearly paralyzes me, like the heavy beat of a drum deep in my belly, growing impossibly stronger with every hard drive of his cock. I can feel my whole body tighten around him.

He brings our chests together and fists my hair in one hand, causing a slight sting. "Can you feel me now, baby?"

"Oh my God, yes." My fingernails dig deeper into his hot flesh. My eyes close and roll back at once. I twine my limbs around him, as if I might fly away if I don't hold on.

He doesn't say a word. He doesn't slow down or ease up. I don't want him to.

Every punishing thrust bumps his pelvis against my clit. Enough to remind me of the orgasm he licked me toward, enough to make his cock inside me all the more intense, but not enough to push me over.

"Please... please..." I say the word over and over, like a chant in time to his rough drives. Like a prayer asking for all the things he's promised me since coming back into my life.

"Tell me what you want." He caresses my cheek on his way to my nape, using his grasp there as leverage to fuck me harder.

I'm not sure how to ask for what I want. I'm reaching for something more, something nameless that feels just out of reach. I'm trembling. I can barely breathe, let alone give him a coherent answer. I feel fractured, cut up between all the sensations he's inspired, but never pulled completely under. And that's what I need.

"Make me come. Please... Kase..."

He lowers his head and kisses me roughly. "Love when you beg," he rasps, his breath hot against my lips. Only then do I notice the sweat beading along his brow and the tense line of his jaw.

When he lowers his hand between us and strokes my clit, my whole body tenses.

"Jesus Christ," he mutters, closing his eyes.

Stars dance in my vision. The combination of his cock pounding into me and his fingers working their magic are too much and everything and not enough all at once. Every cell in my body reaches for climax.

When his eyes open again, I'm lost, reeling. The rapture sweeping his features is more than my heart can handle.

"June..."

Our lips brush. We breathe each other's air. The orgasm is a hurricane of sensation, more powerful than I'd ever realized could be possible. It takes me under, and I cry out. A long, hoarse sound that mingles with his as I lock down tightly onto him.

He stills inside me, thick and deep and pulsing, and for one lucid moment, I hate the condom between us.

He rests his forehead against mine. Our ragged breathing fills the air. Our bodies are slick with sweat and arousal. Little shocks of pleasure ripple through me, as if my body can't let go of the feeling all at once. I wish I never had to give it up at all...

"Thank you," I say, emotion knotting inside me.

He shakes his head slightly. His chest still heaves as he catches his breath. Taking my hand, he kisses my fingertips and drags them down, molding my palm against his racing heart.

My own twists. Every second takes me down from the physical high, but another kind of high takes its place. The warm buzz of Kase in my world transcends the physical. And now I worry I may have given him more than my body.

I may have just given up my heart.

★ ★ ★ ★

Sweat cools on my skin as I stare at Kase's bedroom ceiling. Locusts chirp through the window. I can hear the shower in the hallway bathroom running. As the water crashes intermittently, I imagine Kase soaping up his glorious body. I should be in there doing it for him. I said I'd join him in a few minutes, but I seem paralyzed here. I can still feel him everywhere—the rhythm of our lovemaking, his gentle strength, the nearly blinding orgasm that tore through me.

I draw in a deep breath, sit up, and swing my legs off the side of the bed. I run my fingers through my tangled hair and shiver when a cool mountain breeze flows inside. Kase is probably wondering where I am, but I'm too in my head right now. What happened between us has me undeniably shaken. My muscles are weak, and I worry that my legs won't carry me downstairs. But I need air. I need to think...

I pull on my shorts and T-shirt, not bothering with anything else, and head downstairs. I open the fridge and quickly decide I'm not hungry. I grab a glass from the cupboard and go to the living room, where I'd noticed a liquor shelf earlier today. The half-empty bottle of Angel's Envy catches my eye. I'll be twenty-one in a few months, and my father has always trusted me to use discretion when it came to an occasional drink. So I pour a couple fingers of the amber liquid, trying not to think about how Julie remembered Kase's drink of choice a few days ago. What irritated me before burns me now. I don't want anyone knowing Kase the way I do.

God, I need to get a grip. How did I get here so fast? From being eager to fulfill my father's dream of expanding the hotel grounds to falling hard and fast for my high school crush? To the point where I can't imagine not having him in my life now. I can't stomach the idea of anyone else looking at him and thinking they could have him the way I just did.

I go to the back porch and take my spot on the swing again. The night is navy blue, nearly black. Fireflies sprinkle little bursts of yellow light across the field. I sip my liquor, hoping it calms my racing thoughts and fierce feelings for Kase.

Why did tonight have to be so perfect? No one's first time is this good. I've heard enough horror stories from the girls at work to know this. Why does Kase have to fuck like a dream? I already want more. And after the aggressive way he took me, my body has no business craving another round so soon.

"Hey." Kase, wearing only a fresh pair of jeans, steps out on the porch, his hair still wet from the shower.

"Hi," I say as he approaches.

He sits on the other side of the bench. "Are you all right?"

I take a deep breath. "I'm fine."

"You disappeared on me. Now I find you here drinking hard liquor. Something's wrong."

I laugh softly. "I just experienced the most intense orgasm of my life. I'm...a little overwhelmed. I just needed some air."

His shoulders soften. He takes my legs and turns me so they drape over his thighs and I face him. He strokes my calves in silence for a moment. "You sure that's all?"

He takes my glass and brings it to his lips, never breaking eye contact. Swallowing, he touches my wrists, still pink from where he held me firmly earlier. "Was I too rough?"

"You were perfect. You're an amazing lover. Everything I imagined you could be and more. I think that's what's terrifying me right now. I don't want to feel so..."

I take the glass back and swallow my next thought with the burning liquid. I drain the glass and set it to the side, praying for clarity. I'm pretty sure Kase obliterated any chance of that, though.

"I don't want to be that girl who confuses an amazing physical experience for something more. I'm just finding it a little difficult right now."

He frowns. "I just made love to you. It was incredible, for both of us. And now you're trying to talk yourself out of feeling emotional about it?"

I sigh. "Basically."

"Then what's the point?"

I meet his confused frown. "We have an arrangement, Kase. A business deal, and I have to remember that's what this is about."

All humor flees his features. He looks down, his lips tight, before meeting my eyes again. "Is that what you think this is about, June? Business?"

No. But I'm not ready to fall in love with you...

I shake my head, running from the dangerous thought. "Everything's mixed up right now."

He takes my hand, rubbing his thumb over my knuckles. "That's how life gets sometimes."

I sigh again, and he pulls me toward him so I'm settled on his lap. I relax in the warmth of his arms. He kisses the top of my head when I lean into his broad chest.

"How about we enjoy each other for the rest of the time we have and not worry about what it all means? Just let ourselves do whatever feels right, feel what we want to feel, even if it's a little scary, and trust that things will sort themselves out in the end."

He's saying what I want to hear. Letting myself disappear in the moment with him and forgetting the consequences of what we do here is tempting. The way things are going, I don't ever want this time with him to end, so I'm willing to pretend it won't.

I feather my fingertips across his bare chest, memorizing every contour as I go. "Okay."

But a seed of fear takes root beside my optimism. The further I fall, the more I stand to risk.

He touches my chin, guiding my gaze to his. "Tonight was about more than money and land. I've wanted this as long as you have. You need to know that."

The look in his eyes leaves no doubt. I believe him. I just don't trust the way we feel about each other will lead anywhere good when this is all done. But when he kisses me again, slowly, tenderly, all I know is the here and now. And right now, he's everything. And there is no end.

When I break away to catch a breath, we're entwined and panting. He's hard beneath me, and I'm rubbing against him like a cat in heat. Jesus, how can I want him again already? Then it occurs to me that I haven't cleaned up since our last round.

"I should shower," I say, leaning away.

He hums and pulls me back. "Nah. You smell like sex and biscuits. I love it." With his arms wrapped around me, he licks my neck, sucking on a spot below my ear that gives me goosebumps.

I giggle and push on his chest. "Knock it off. Let me get cleaned up."

He groans and finally releases me from his embrace. "You're right. We should get some rest. I have to get up early, and you'll be sore if I take you again tonight."

I bite my lip and regret that he's probably right. I'm already a little sore, but I'm willing to ignore that to feel him moving over me again. As long as we're pretending we have forever, though...

I bring us chest-to-chest, lose myself in another kiss, and convince myself this truly never has to end.

CHAPTER ELEVEN

Last night fulfilled all my fantasies about being intimate with Kase. We'd fallen asleep in each other's arms, and I'd slept as soundly as I ever had. But waking up to an empty bed makes me miss him in a way that nearly hurts in its intensity.

On his pillow rests a note and a tiny bouquet of wildflowers. I bring them to my nose, inhaling the sweet aromas. I push up to my elbows and unfold the note.

June Bell, the girl who makes my dreams come true...

I could hardly bring myself to leave you this morning. I think I could watch you sleep for hours. Thank you for a night I'll never forget and for letting me wake up to you in my arms.

See you tonight. (Let me help with dinner.)

Kase

I roll to my back and hold the note to my chest. I'm hardly awake and my heart is tripping. I close my eyes and let the memory of last night wash over me. Kase was, in a word, *perfect*. He was slow and tender. Careful and sweet. Then he was so much more. The way he transformed, knowing what I needed without me even knowing it myself, was so unexpectedly perfect.

How on earth am I going to survive an entire day without seeing him? I glance at the clock. It's nearly ten. Kase gets up at the crack of dawn, so he could be ready for lunch soon enough.

Another day spent inside missing Kase will be nothing short of torture, so I decide today's the day to start seeing the McCasker farm past these walls. I've scarcely left the house since arriving.

I jump up and get dressed. I choose a red sundress and a pair of worn leather boots. I toss my hair up into a ponytail and put on a little makeup, even though I've been wearing a permanent flush all morning. Every time I think of last night with Kase, my body temperature skyrockets.

Downstairs I make a plan for dinner while I sip my coffee, trying not to let my thoughts wander. I put Kase's flowers in a little vase on the counter and mill around the house, spotting an old basket by the door that will be perfect for a picnic lunch if I can steal Kase away from his work. Emptying it of magazines and junk mail that have accumulated, I bring it to the kitchen and pack sandwiches, fruit, drinks, and a blanket.

It's just past eleven when I can't bring myself to kill any more time waiting. I need to see Kase.

Outside, the summer air is mild. The sun is warm on my bare shoulders, and the breeze is just enough to cut the heat. I journey through the large field in the back of the house toward the bright-red barn in the distance. Behind it are several more buildings, flanked by two silos.

At the first building I reach, I peek inside, hoping to find Kase. My heart leaps when I see someone sweeping out one of the dozens of stalls that line the long room. I can't see his face under his hat.

"Kase?" I walk deeper inside.

The man looks up and turns my way. He's not Kase. He's dressed head to toe in denim that matches his smiling blue eyes. "Can I help you?"

"I was looking for Kase. Is he around?"

"He's been in the office for a couple hours. Want me to get him for you?"

"If you can point me in the right direction, I'll bring him his lunch." I lift the picnic basket.

The man grins and leans on the broom. "Well, well. That's nice of you. What's the occasion?"

I shrug and look down, knowing my cheeks are probably as red as my dress. "Just lunch."

He comes toward me in a few strides, slipping off his glove before extending his hand. "I'm Chad, by the way. I help out around here a few days a week. You must be the new lady of the house."

I shake his hand. He's taller than Kase, a short blond fuzz covering his head. "Nice to meet you, Chad. I'm June. I'm just staying with Kase for a little while."

He nods and gives me a quick once-over before averting his eyes. "You two an item?"

I laugh nervously. "Something like that."

What are we? Is Kase my "boyfriend," or are these two weeks a fling that's destined to end when my father buys the land? That familiar feeling of dread settles over me, but I push it away. I don't have to think about that yet. Our time isn't up, and as long as I'm here, I'm determined to make the most of it.

"He's a lucky guy," Chad says with a wink. He points to the door

I came through. "The office is in the next building over, in the back. Don't make him too late. I need him back here to milk the cows at three."

I laugh and turn for the door. "I won't keep him too long. Good to meet you."

"You too, June."

I leave and enter another building with a similar layout. The stalls are already clean and everything seems in order. In the back, there's a door with a shiny silver sign that reads Office. I knock.

"Come in." Kase's voice is muffled on the other side.

I open the door slowly. He's seated behind a metal desk, its surface covered with paperwork. Behind him are several filing cabinets and shelves overflowing with binders and folders. He doesn't look up when I enter.

"What do you need, Chad?"

I clear my throat.

He lifts his gaze, and his jaw drops a little. "Oh hell."

I smirk. "I brought you lunch."

He slams closed what looks like an executive checkbook and pushes away from the desk. He rounds it and comes to me. I expect him to say something, but he takes the basket from me, drops it to the floor, and folds his arms around me. Then his lips are sealed over mine. A small moan leaves my lips and disappears between our mouths.

He kisses me like we've been apart for days, not hours. I curl my arms around him and return it with all I have.

"I missed you," he whispers when we break apart.

"I missed you too." I look deeply into his eyes, and in that moment I ache to tell him how much he's beginning to mean to me.

Before I can consider it, he leans down and grabs the basket. "Come on. Let's get out of here."

He takes my hand and leads me outside. We walk for several minutes across a hilly pasture toward a patch of trees. As we get closer, I recognize the small unripe fruit clinging to the branches.

"You have an apple orchard?"

"Just a small one. Enough to sell some produce at the farmers market for a few weeks in the fall."

He leads us to a shady spot between two trees. "Here good?"

"Perfect." I reach into the basket. "I hoped we could eat outside. I brought a blanket just for this."

I shake out the folds and the breeze ripples the material before it settles on the grass. I sit on the edge and unpack our lunch. "Are you hungry?"

Kase lays behind me, feathering his touch up my spine and kissing my arm. "I'm starving." His tone is low and suggestive. "I don't usually eat during the day. You're spoiling me."

I turn toward him with a frown. "You don't? That's crazy. You need to eat, Kase. Especially with how hard you work." I shake my head. "I'll start making you lunch."

He pushes me to the blanket with a growl. I'm sprawled on my back as he covers my body with the perfect weight of his. His thigh rests between my legs, and his lips journey up and down the column of my neck.

"Kase." His name escapes my lips, falling somewhere between objection and invitation.

"What?" He flickers his tongue over my collarbone.

That quickly I'm consumed. Wrapped in his heat, drowning in his touch, aching for more of everything. I fist my hands to keep from grabbing at him. "Aren't we going to eat?"

"Maybe later," he says against my skin. "You didn't expect to show up here like Little Red Riding Hood and not let me eat you, did you?"

My breath rushes out of me.

Fine. To hell with lunch.

I arch against his mouth as it comes over my breast. He brings his teeth firmly around my hardened nipple through the cotton, making me whimper and sigh. I'm learning to love the unexpected rush of his touch. The way he takes me right to the edge, right to the place where I think my limit is, only to make me fly past it in a matter of seconds. I sift my fingers through his hair and move my hips. Rubbing myself on his thigh, I drag my heel up his calf.

He slides his hand up my leg, reaches between us, and teases his fingertips over my panties.

"*Why* are you wearing panties?"

His eyes are dead serious, but I can't help but giggle.

"Just think of the things I could do to you if these panties weren't in the way. I could feel how wet you are for me."

I bite my lip and buck slightly into his slow, torturous slides against me.

"I could sink into you," he whispers, delving his tongue into my mouth, dueling with mine. "Could make you come right here."

"Bad habit, I guess," I say, overwhelmed with the visions that come with his lusty threats.

He nips at my lips. "I think I can break you of it."

Suddenly, he rolls me to my belly and lifts my dress up past my hips. The rough feel of his palms against the backs of my thighs prickles my desire. I don't know what he has planned for me, but that makes me want it even more.

Then the sound of his hand on my ass slices through the air. A hard slap that steals my breath. Instinct drives me to protect myself. I bring my hand to the place where he made contact, the skin already searing. He grabs my wrist and pins it against the small of my back.

"Kase," I say breathlessly. "What are you doing?"

He massages my sore bottom, cupping and squeezing my cheek in his palm. "Teaching you a lesson."

The pain is sobering. I'm no longer lost in the haze of lust. I'm tempted to squirm away and let him know what a good hard slap feels like, when his mouth touches my skin. He traces his tongue along the edge of my panties, slowly, until all I can feel is his warm breath against my pussy through the fabric. Okay, panties truly are an evil invention.

The anger that boiled within me moments ago has reduced to a simmer I can't separate from my desire. My hips seem to move on their own, lifting, seeking more warm temptations from Kase's mouth.

"You want me to do that again?"

I tense, bracing myself for it. "It hurts."

"Yeah," he says, lowering to kiss and lick against the pulsing heat. "Then what does it feel like?"

I shake my head, because I'm all mixed up. I'm uncomfortable but still impossibly turned on somehow.

I want to turn you on so much it hurts.

His fingertips press against the wetness in my panties. I push back against him with a moan. I don't know why I want it, but I do.

"Do it," I say, flinging the last of my worry into the wind.

"You sure?"

"Ye—"

His hand comes down, no softer than before. I bite my lip to suppress a whimper as he begins the same treatment on the other burning cheek. Warm, soft kisses. Trails of his tongue that cool in the open air. My God, if anyone were to find us out here...

"You going to wear panties anymore?"

"No. Never," I say quickly.

He's made his point. Underwear has never been a hindrance for him before, but now he's honoring the barrier with a conviction that makes me want to scream in frustration. The way I ache for his mouth and touch everywhere I'm covered is all the reason I need to ditch them for the rest of time.

"Good girl," he says, flipping me back.

Sunlight dances through the branches in the apple trees above us. He wears a hungry stare, a dark-gray T-shirt, and blue jeans. His erection strains against the zipper. I reach for him, but he catches my hand.

"Wait."

My eyes widen. "Wait for what?"

A smile curves his lips. "Patience, June. I wasn't expecting you. I need to get a condom from the house. Can you wait for me?"

I hesitate a moment. "You don't have to. I've been on the pill," I say.

His smile fades. "Why didn't you tell me before?"

I swallow. "It's more intimate. I had to be sure I wanted that with you."

"Do you?"

The minute he came last night, I knew I didn't want anything between us again. I nod. "I do."

He lowers down over me, kissing me softly. "I know it pisses you off, but I haven't been living as a monk. I've always been safe, though."

I tense beneath him. He's right. The thought of him being with another woman makes me crazy. I try not to dwell on that. Instead, I let the idea of him being inside me take over. I reach for the button on his jeans again, and this time he lets me unzip him.

Then I hear someone yelling. We freeze, staring at each other and then in the direction of the sound. In the distance I see the shrunken figure of a man in the field behind the house. Then another yell. It sounds like my name.

I push Kase away and scramble to sit up. "Oh my God. It's my dad."

CHAPTER TWELVE

Shit.

The closer I get to Daddy, the deeper the panic sets in. He's coming toward me and Kase as quickly as we're approaching. He's got murder in his eyes, and his arms are swinging wildly at his sides.

"Daddy," I say in my calmest tone when we meet in the middle of the field. "What are you doing here?"

He shoves his finger at Kase, who slows behind me. "You better not have laid a finger on her."

My mouth falls agape slightly. I've rarely had cause to lie to my father, but this seems like a good time to start if it eases the tension rippling off him.

"Daddy, what are you talking about?"

He slides his angry gaze to me. "I went into town for some shopping, and do you know what I hear? I hear that Kase McCasker's got some girl half naked in his truck down by the Conway Ledge trails. Is that true?"

I swallow hard. *Shit. Shit. Shit.* When I can't form a reply, the color in his cheeks rises to a fierce red. He looks back to Kase, whose face is an unreadable mask.

"That's what this was about? You thought you'd take advantage of my daughter, as what, a perk of the deal? Or were you planning to send her back after you had your way with her and foil the deal? Is Edwin behind this?"

Kase slides his hand into mine. "June came here of her own free will."

"And you're making a whore out of her! June, you're coming home with me. Pack your things. Now."

My father's words hit me like a slap to the face. Tears burn behind my eyes. Kase squeezes my hand, and the small show of support eases the pain a fraction.

"If she goes, there's no deal," Kase says quietly.

My father regards him with more malice than I've ever seen. "Surely there's something you want more than her company for another week."

Kase's jaw is firm, the muscles there bulging as he clenches.

"Five percent," my father says. "I'll bump the price up by five percent. I'll chalk it up to inflation with the investors."

My jaw falls. "Daddy!"

Kase's stance and expression haven't changed.

"If she goes," he says with control, "there's no deal, Mr. Bell. You could offer me double, and that wouldn't change. My terms were clear. I'm not renegotiating."

"Bastard!" Daddy's face is beet red. Sweat crowns his forehead. He's in his requisite blazer, but he looks ragged, like he could turn violent at any time. He comes closer, until he's only a few inches from Kase. "One day everyone in Falls Edge will know who you are."

He turns away from us both and marches toward the house. I follow after him, leaving Kase behind.

"Daddy, wait. Please."

After several paces, he finally slows. I circle in front of him, but he doesn't meet my gaze. He rubs the sweat off with a handkerchief from his breast pocket. "How could you let this happen, June?"

I wince. Of all the ways I agonized over the potential pitfalls of this arrangement with Kase, I never expected this.

I laugh roughly. "What did you expect was going to happen? You sent me off without a second thought. All you cared about was getting the deal in motion again."

"Don't put this on me." He points his finger and his weary gaze at me.

Tears pool at the corners of my eyes, but I don't want to break down right now. Because Kase is right. I chose to come here. And I'm not ready to leave yet.

His expression softens. "June." He sighs. "Just come back to the hotel. The land... I'll make Edwin see reason. They want to sell. I'm sure of it. Everything he's said this week points in that direction. They're feeling the financial pressure more than ever. Even with Kase back, they may be too far behind to catch up. Hell, I can probably get it for *less* than the original bargain."

I can't believe what he's saying. "I'm not leaving."

He frowns, seemingly unaware of the tears streaming down my cheeks now. "You *want* to stay here?"

I swallow hard. "I care about him."

He shakes his head. "June, no. This dalliance—whatever is going on between you two—can't continue. I'm *not* losing you to a McCasker."

"You're not losing me." I stifle a sob, but they're getting harder to hold back.

His anger is back, flaring behind his eyes and stiffening his posture. "Do I have to go in there and pack your things myself? Just come back home, and we can talk this all out. You think you know that boy, but believe me, you don't."

"I'm a grown woman. I agreed to stay here with Kase, and that's what I'm going to do. I'll come home when I'm ready."

"Goddamnit." He paces a few steps away and turns toward Kase, who's standing stoic in the field, watching us.

"What did they ever do to you to make you hate them so much?"

Daddy's jacket moves as he inhales. "They took something precious from me. And I'm not going to stand idly by and watch them do it again." He turns back to me, his expression grim. "You want to stay here, June? Fine. But mark my words. As soon as this land is mine, you're not going anywhere near Kase McCasker. There's nothing negotiable about that."

As he walks away, I can feel something inside me breaking. Not my heart. Something deeper, more foundational. I've never been at odds like this with my father. But no matter how much I want to please him, I can't bring myself to follow him back to the hotel. At least for now, I'm rooted here. With Kase.

I watch my father peel down the road, leaving nothing but dust and his anger lingering.

Kase comes behind me, gently placing his hands on my arms. "You okay?"

A sob rips out of me. I turn and bury my face in his shirt. We hold each other tight, and while I relish the comfort of the embrace, my father's words echo through me over and over again, tearing a painful path every time.

You're making a whore out of her.

I pull from Kase's arms and wipe my face. "I need to be alone right now."

He frowns. "Let me stay with you. I can take the afternoon off. Chad can cover for me for the rest of the day."

I shake my head and sniffle. "No. I'm fine. You can go back. I'll see you tonight."

I take strides toward the house, grateful when he doesn't follow me. I don't know why, but I long for the comfort of Kase's bed and the quiet house. No prying eyes. No chatter. No responsibilities tugging at me.

Even though I feel ripped apart, I'm glad it's happened here, in a place that's beginning to feel more like home than my room at the hotel. Far away from my father's judgments and blind ambition. He's never felt more like a stranger to me, and for a moment, I wonder if being here has changed me so much, or if he's only now showing how ugly his hatred for the McCaskers truly is.

I climb the stairs and slip under Kase's quilt, letting the tears run down the sides of my face. I pull his pillow into my arms and breathe in his scent. I miss him. As much as I wish he were here comforting me, I don't want him to see me this way.

With every breath, I try to let go of my father's words. I sink into calm, comforted by the smell of the man I'm falling hard and fast for and the quiet house that's letting me simply be. Then I let sleep take its hold.

I wake several hours later to the sounds of dishes clanging in the kitchen. I rise and try to tame my bed head in the mirror that rests atop Kase's dresser. My eyes are puffy, but the uncontrollable urge to cry until I have nothing left is over. The sun has set, and the sky is a darkening violet. Time has passed, and for now, my father's words have lost enough of their potency that I can face Kase again.

He's in the kitchen chopping vegetables and sprinkling them over a large bowl of salad. He looks up when I enter the room.

"Hey," he says softly. He looks relaxed, but his eyes are filled with worry.

I join him at the counter and peek into the large pot filled with his favorite boxed macaroni and cheese. I can't help but smile at the orange concoction.

"You really need to expand your repertoire."

He smirks. "It works in a pinch. And I branched out. I made a side salad."

"Looks good," I say, popping a slice of celery into my mouth. "Do you need help with anything?"

"I think everything is ready. Are you hungry?"

I nod. "Starving. I haven't eaten all day."

His brows wrinkle, but he moves quickly, makes us plates, and brings them to the dining room. We sit and begin to eat in silence. I'm famished, but as Kase's dinner satisfies my hunger, all the things we aren't saying—things my father said that I can't stop thinking about—begin to weigh on me.

I want to be here with Kase, but only for the right reasons.

I set my fork down on my empty plate and contemplate what to say. "Kase, I think we should talk."

He leans back in his chair. "Yeah."

I sigh because I don't know where to start. "My father..."

He works his jaw and traces the edge of the table. "If I hear him talk to you like that again, June, I'm not sure I'm going to be able to control myself. Is that how he is with you?"

"No. He's angry sometimes, but I've never seen him like that. I think all of this—*us*—is sending him over the edge. I'm his only child."

"You're not a whore, and if anyone dares call you that again, they're going to get introduced to my fist."

I swallow over the emotion thick in my throat. "Why did he warn me about you? It's like he hates you as much as he hates your father."

The silence that stretches between us only adds to my unease. Kase doesn't make eye contact. Only now do I realize he hasn't touched me since I came downstairs. The physical and emotional space between us feeds all my doubts about being here.

I stand to leave, when he catches my hand.

"Don't go."

His gaze travels from our joined hands to the old, worn table and back to me. I ease back down into my chair.

"I've never told anyone this," he says softly.

My heart starts to hammer a little faster. I hold my breath and wait for him to speak.

"Your mom died when you were a baby, June. No one had to tell you when it happened. It's how it always was."

Confused, I nod.

"I know that doesn't make not having your mother any easier," he says. "But you never had to deal with the shock and try to work it out in your head."

"What are you saying, Kase?"

"Edwin," he says, his gaze floating up to the lilies spilling out of the vase on the table. "He's not my father."

CHAPTER THIRTEEN

"What?" My eyes go wide. The air in my lungs exits from the pure shock of Kase's confession.

"But... Your mother. If she left—"

He lets go of my hand.

"Lily McCasker wasn't some woman Edwin knocked up who took off after she gave birth to me. She was his sister, and he took her in." He swallows and clasps his hands on the table, his focus fixed on the brilliant orange blossoms in front of us. "She was following a band around the country. Fell for the guitarist and ended up getting pregnant. She was hopelessly in love with the guy, but when she had the baby...*me*. Well, life on the road wasn't a life for a newborn. So she came home."

"But you said she left."

"Edwin said he'd help support us until she could get on her feet. But she was barely here a week before her old life called her back."

He exhales heavily. His eyes are calm, serious, as if maybe he's found peace with the tragedy of his parentage.

"She left me with Edwin. Said she'd come back as soon as she convinced my father to settle down with her. Somehow, Edwin knew that wasn't going to happen, so he decided right then to raise me as his own. In a small town, he figured it was the best thing. He was probably right, but I couldn't accept any of that when he told me."

"When did you find out?"

"Your father came to him with the offer when I had one foot out the door for college. He had your dad's proposal in his hand when he told me. It wasn't long after that night with you at the falls. He was worried about keeping things up after I left. Said he didn't feel right selling it without my blessing, because the land could be mine one day. Whether or not I was his true son, I would inherit everything. But he fed me a lie for eighteen years."

"Edwin cares for you. I know he does."

His painful grimace breaks through the calm he'd shown before. I reach for his hand and hold it firmly.

"There probably never would have been a good time to tell me the truth. But I had my whole life ahead of me, June, and then it was like nothing made sense. How could any of it matter when both my fucking parents abandoned me? I mean, I'd grown up making up stories about my mom, trying to rationalize why she left. But *both* of them?"

The well of emotion within me inches to the surface again, and my heart breaks for the truth we both now know. "I'm sorry, Kase."

He shakes his head, a faraway look in his eyes. "He made me believe I was someone I wasn't. I was devastated. More lost than I've ever felt in my life. Half dead, half trying to live. I told him to sell it. Have a nice life."

"But he didn't sell," I say.

"I left early for school. Found an apartment and a job to help me with expenses. I only came home when I had to. But we never talked about it again. I just figured the deal fell through somehow. I think he was waiting for me to change my mind all this time."

Suddenly Kase's absence makes perfect sense, and I feel worse for holding it against him when he had his own burden to bear.

"But you came back to stay," I say softly.

He turns his blue-eyed gaze my way. "Because I'm done looking backward for answers. There's nothing there, June. I spent four years trying to wrestle some kind of control over my past. Nothing changes the fact that the two people who put me here don't give a damn. All I can do is look ahead and try to create something better. Something real that no one can tear away."

"Here?"

He blinks and looks down at our joined hands. "That was the idea."

Tears brim my eyes. I pull away to wipe at them. "Kase, why? Why did you agree to this with me?"

I push up from the table and walk through the house until fresh air hits me on the back porch. I want to keep walking. Through the field. Into the night and solitude of the mountains. I'd give anything to be at the falls right now, the steady rush of water drowning out my thoughts and dulling the pain.

But an invisible force pins me to the porch when I hear Kase's footsteps behind me.

Suddenly I remembered Edwin's words the day I came here. *I just hope you're doing this for the right reasons, June. I'm not entirely sure Kase is.*

He's spun this web and trapped me here with this twisted deal. I should be running from him, but I ache to be in his arms. To hold him through his pain and let him chase away mine. Tears stream down my cheeks as I search for answers that seem impossible and so far out of reach.

I can feel his heat as he comes near, his presence like the pulse of my own heart. I grip my hands around my arms to keep from collapsing into the comfort of his.

"June, don't be angry with me," he says. "Look at me. Talk to me."

I suck in a shaky breath and turn to face him. For all the dominance he's shown me since coming back into my life, he's showing me something different now. There's something raw and vulnerable about the way he looks at me, like somehow I hold power over him now.

I brush at my tears, but they just keep coming. And I thought I'd cried all I could today. "Kase... Why did you do this? You brought me here and made me feel things for you. You promised me a dream at the expense of your own. Why?"

He cradles my cheeks in his hands. "Because I saw you again, and for a split second I remembered the person I was before my life went to hell. I remembered how that night felt between us. I remembered a hundred little moments when I'd wanted to talk to you and know you but held back. The past four years faded away, like some kind of terrible penance that I'd paid and could finally let go of. God help me, I saw you and everything made sense."

I close my eyes, pushing more tears down my cheeks. "But the house...the land."

"June," he whispers.

I sigh into the barest brush of his lips over mine and blink my eyes open. I yearn to be consumed. Taken under, swept so far away from the truth and the reality I now have to face. But he draws back, gazing deeply into my eyes.

"When I came home, I promised to give myself time to figure out whether to stay or leave for good. I could go make a life somewhere else far away from Falls Edge, or I could stay and try to turn the farm into something more than it has been. I could start over, or I could put down roots and make something real, something stronger than the lie I grew up on." He hesitates, his lips parted gently. "I had to give us a chance, June."

A chance...

So simple. Such a pure possibility, full of hope and the kinds of moments we've shared these past couple days. But nothing is simple now. How could it ever be?

"At the risk of your family's future? Did you once think about what it meant to put that on me? I'm caught in the middle of this."

I pull back, fresh anger mingling with my confusion and hurt. I glance out at the moon, a gauzy white against the violet sky.

"Maybe I should just go," I say softly. "Being here with you is killing my father. And, honestly, I don't know what's going to be left of me if I stay."

"That's not the answer."

His tone is clipped. If I could see his face, I'm certain I'd see his determination to make me stay. I'm certain I'd be powerless to deny him.

I close my eyes a moment. "We can't keep doing this, Kase. Everything has changed."

"What's changed?"

His tone is so measured I can sense immediately that he's

preparing to change my mind.

"You love this house, and this is your life now," I say. "I won't be the one to take it from you. If you and Edwin decide to sell, it's between you and my father. I won't be caught in the middle of it. It's not fair."

He's quiet a moment. "It may not be fair, but it's what we all agreed to."

I look away, my hopelessness intensifying at the prospect of leaving the farm to save Kase's dream. What would I do then? Try to soften the blow of disappointment when my father realizes the deal is off? Figure out how to keep building on the relationship that's formed between Kase and me? Best case, my father accepts both in time. Worst case, his grudge against the McCaskers deepens and he makes a future with Kase unbearable.

"I don't know what to do," I whisper, trying like hell to keep my emotions in check.

"Stay." Kase takes my hand in his. "I'll admit that I manipulated the situation to get closer to you, but I also wanted you to get to know the property better. Your father's not the only one who wants the expansion to happen. You believe in it too, right?"

I sigh. "Well...I mean, yes. But I was believing in it before I realized what this meant to you. This is your life."

"If losing it all brings me you, I think I could live with it."

I frown. "You can't mean that."

"Believe it. Why the hell do you think I put it all on the line?"

"But you don't have to. I can go home—"

"Hell no." He pulls me against his hard body in one swift move. The low, growly demand makes my insides quiver.

"You're staying, June. Right here, in my bed, in this home, for the time we agreed to. And if handing it all over to your father at the end of it is what I have to do to be with you, then that's what I'll do. Because if you go back to the hotel right now, it's over. He'll make seeing each other impossible. We'll have to sneak around to be together, because you love him and you'll want to protect him. He'll hate me until his dying breath, and you know it."

Everything he's saying makes sense, but none of it can convince me that tearing away his home and his dreams will ever be worth it. "Kase, I can't let you do this deal."

"I don't fucking care about the deal. Right now, all I care about is you."

He's as beautiful as ever, even more so wearing the look of possession that's tightened his features.

I open my mouth to argue, but his lips are on me before I can speak. He's warm and soft, but his kiss is fierce, almost bruising in its intensity. Every sweep of his tongue against mine steals away my reason. He moves his hands over me, every firm grasp like an echo of his early insistence that I stay.

And, damn it, no part of me wants to leave. I worry that'll never change...

I meet his fervor, regretting the clothes that keep our skin from touching everywhere. He nips at my lips, tiny pinpricks of pain that match his passion. I slide my fingers through his hair, tugging at the roots, and count the steps between the place where we stand and the bedroom.

Need him. Need him now...

As if he hears my silent begging, we stumble into the house. We never stop touching, kissing, reaching for more. I claw at his shirt, desperate to get it off him. He manages to yank it off, tripping us as we reach the bottom step of the stairs. When I fall backward, he follows me down.

He pushes my dress up to my waist and grinds his hips against my center. The sound that carries past my lips can't be me. It's feral and desperate before disappearing into another fierce kiss. My skin prickles everywhere we touch, everywhere I badly need his hands on me.

Nothing about our position is especially comfortable, but I'm frantic to have him inside me. I've never been this turned on in my life. Last night was a craving made up of years of fantasies. This is different. This is desperate, because now I know the heaven of our bodies joined.

Unwilling to prolong the torture, I reach for the button on his jeans and unzip him free. He's hard and hot to the touch, velvet over steel as I stroke him to the tip. I look into his eyes, which have gone molten.

With both hands, he grips the narrow strip of panties along my hip.

"Last warning about these," he mutters, baring a hint of teeth as the fabric rips. He repeats the motion on the other side before tossing the ruined garment away.

Fisting his cock, he guides it up and down my slit. His blatant appraisal of me sends a rush of heat to my cheeks. But I can't feel shy when he's staring at me like this, like I'm all he's ever needed. He tantalizes my clit with short, teasing strokes from the plush head and solid length of his cock.

"Kase..."

I curl my fingers around the baluster and spread my legs wider, begging with my body for what we both so badly need. He drifts lower, pressing into flesh still tender from the night before. He's barely penetrating me, but the hint of connection has me dizzy.

I try to hook my heels behind his thighs, but he catches my knees and presses me wide. Another desperate moan threatens to break free. His sudden restraint is unfathomable to me.

"Don't move," he says, his eyelids heavy with lust. "Let me appreciate you this way."

I still, eager but equally willing to savor the new sensation of being with him bare.

He traps his bottom lip between his teeth, hissing softly as he pushes a centimeter farther. "Are you sure? Because I'm not sure I can stop now. Feels too damn good already."

"I've never been more sure of anything, Kase. Please..."

CHAPTER FOURTEEN

With that small consent, he leans in until I'm sure I've stretched to accommodate every inch of him. He punches his hips forward. The sudden move to claim even more space robs me of breath.

"Fuck," he breathes into the space between us. "You okay?"

"Yes... My God, yes." I close my eyes and reach for control I no longer have. I'm trembling in my effort not to move, not to cry out and beg for more. But that's what I want. *More. Harder. Faster. Please... Please.*

"Say it again," he rasps.

I blink up at him. Only then do I realize I muttered the pleas out loud as they rang through my thoughts. He withdraws to the tip and lingers there, waiting.

"More," I whisper.

The slow thrust that follows lets me feel every ridge of his cock, every inch of his possession. I'm convinced in this moment that I'll never tire of the feel of him...of this. The sweetest torture.

My lip trembles. "Harder."

He pulls back and slams his hips forward again.

"Ah!" The stair treads dig into my back with the pressure. But the deep, satisfying pleasure thrumming in my core offsets the minor discomfort. My thoughts tumble and whirl, ending with the same chanting plea.

More. More. More.

"More. Kase, I need more."

So much more.

Still, he hesitates.

"Please," I moan.

My knuckles go white around the baluster. I'm ready to wrap myself around him and take control when he leans in and kisses me hard, plunging deep once more.

"Goddamnit." He drags his palms down my calves, guiding my legs around his waist. "I can't do this here and fuck you the way I need to right now."

When he lifts us, he's still deeply embedded in me. I wind my limbs around him and dig my fingernails into his shoulders as he climbs the last few stairs to the landing. I circle my hips, trying desperately to create more friction between us. We're a few steps from the bedroom, but every second it'll take to get there seems impossibly long.

He must be wired to the same clock, because instead of taking me to the bedroom, he pins me against the hallway wall with a thud. "What am I going to do with you?"

"I think you know."

I tug sharply at his hair, and he jerks his hips up, driving hard and deep. I cry out and lasso my limbs tighter around him. I'm lost in the fervent rhythm, free-falling into a dizzying bliss.

The way we move together... It's rough. It's passionate. I can't comprehend there was a time when we didn't have this connection. The heat between us builds until we're slick with sweat, molded together like we were made to fit.

"You like that? You like when I make you feel every inch of me?"

I groan and my body clenches around the divine penetration. "I love it."

"Is that all you love?" His heavy question touches my lips with soft puffs of breath. His eyes are hazy with lust and emotion.

As if my senses weren't already being taken on the most intense roller-coaster of my life, his words hit me with more force than his wild fucking. My lips part with a ragged exhale as I try to separate the depth of what he could be saying from the physical magic between us.

Cutting off the moment, he moves us to the bedroom. He slows at the foot of the bed, lowers me down, and pulls out. My efforts to tug him back to me are thwarted when he wrestles my dress over my head. In seconds, he shucks his jeans, baring every final naked inch.

Lying on my back, I can't help but gaze up in wonder at him— the glorious, naked sex god I've chosen to rock my world, all too aware that he too chose me.

He lifts the corner of his lip in a wry smile. "What are you thinking now?"

I giggle, because my thoughts are largely incoherent. "You make it hard to think when we're like this."

"Yeah?" Slowly he draws his hand up the underside of my thigh, all the way down my calf, and lifts my leg to rest on his shoulder. "I'm going to make it a lot harder for you to think about anything but coming in a minute."

Pushing my other knee out, he slips back inside. I bow off the bed with a sigh. Withdrawing slowly but not completely, he skims his palms to my hips. He draws tiny ovals with his thumbs where the bones jut out. Then he presses his fingertips into the meaty flesh behind and forces my pelvis to tilt up toward him. The shift is only awkward until he joins us sharply again.

"Oh!"

I suck in a sharp breath and circle my grip around his flexed forearms. The slow drag of his cock against my inner walls feels nothing like the last stroke. Or the next.

"Oh... Oh my God," I whimper.

Just when I thought nothing could possibly feel better, I'm convinced his cock has just discovered a raw nerve buried in the depths of me. The sensations ricocheting through me are so intense, I can scarcely breathe through my cries and moans of delirious pleasure. My pussy is locked around him. I'm trembling uncontrollably.

"Kase... Kase!"

My back arches off the bed as the orgasm tears through me, like a thousand fingernails down every limb. Warm, hot, electric, summoning the attention of every cell of my being.

Pistoning his hips, Kase creates a fierce rhythm. A little more force each time, until the headboard is knocking on the wall. The lamp on the bedside table is casting jittery shadows across the room. And I don't care if we end up in a pile of rubble if he lets me come again.

Splaying his hand on my belly, he tips his head back. More. Harder. Faster. He gives it all to me. I can't stop begging, crying out his name, clinging to him through every toe-curling climax.

His muscles flex, carving more beautiful shadows into his body.

His torso quakes, and I know he's there.

"June... Baby... Fuck." He flexes his jaw and then releases as a groan pours out.

He stills, his cock pulsing warm inside me. He closes his eyes, as if the sensation is too much.

With a ragged sigh, he climbs over me, keeping us joined. Our skin is on fire, and I've been nearly torn apart by his rough lovemaking, but I relish the weight of his body over mine. His chest and his heartbeat so close.

He kisses my cheek and lazily caresses down my body. "I told you we'd shake the walls."

I grin. "You definitely kept your promise."

He exhales softly. "Are you going to keep yours?"

I turn and search his gaze, somehow even more vulnerable than it was moments ago. I know what he wants before he says it.

"June, I want you to stay." He cups my cheek tenderly. "Promise me you'll stay."

How can I leave when he's taken hold of my heart so quickly? When the promise of a future with him hangs in the balance? How can I leave before we untangle our dreams?

Still hard, he thrusts gently, and we bind ourselves tighter—arms, legs, hearts. It's as if he's expressing the depth of his determination to make me stay, his commitment to this time we've been given.

Embracing it all, I caress every inch of flesh I can reach. Over his shoulders and down his rippled abdominals, slowing just above where our bodies meet so intimately. I squeeze my eyes closed, letting the perfect pressure of Kase's body rule my senses and chase away my fears.

"June," he pleads with a silken whisper. "Please, baby."

Flickering his tongue against my lips, I open for his soft kiss.

"I'll stay," I say into it, meaning it, fearing it, and hoping against all hope that it's the right choice.

★ ★ ★ ★

I wake the next morning the way I have since I arrived. Enjoying the small sounds of nature and the farm at work drifting in through the window. Then a little flutter of excitement spurs me to turn. Only, Kase's pillow is bare. He didn't leave a note.

My heart sinks a little, but I immediately scold myself for wishing for something so trivial. Still, I know I'll never part with the notes he's already written. They've already been stuffed into my suitcase, beside the photo of my parents that I still can't explain.

Last night was different. More than sex. Deeper than the lust that drove us together. I was hoping maybe he'd found words to describe it. Another day, maybe.

I dress and head downstairs, disappointed anew to find the kitchen lacking a note. Maybe he was late and couldn't take the time. A half-empty pot of coffee sits on the counter, though, so I take a mug from the cupboard and pour a steaming cup.

The screen door in the back squeaks, and a second later, Kase appears. He's dressed casually in jeans, a heather-gray T-shirt, and his work boots, coffee in hand. An unexpected hit of relief and happiness washes over me all at once. God, I really am hopeless.

"I thought I heard you come down," he says with a broad smile. He comes close and kisses me. He tastes like the coffee I've yet to savor.

"Why aren't you working?"

His smile fades a little. "Edwin is home. Came back early this morning and was too restless to hang here at the house. He's helping Chad now, so I've got a bit of a break. I thought we could spend the afternoon together."

I blink up at him, my heart speeding up as I try to piece together what could have happened at the hotel. "What did he say? What happened?"

He shrugs and refills his cup to the brim. "I don't know. He seemed aggravated. Didn't want to talk much about it, but from what I can gather, your dad was in a rage after he left here yesterday. I'm guessing he may have taken it out on Edwin. Probably kicked him out or did something that would make another day under his fancy red roof intolerable."

The insult gets under my skin a little, and for the first time since being at the farmhouse, I feel like I'm not where I should be. My father's beyond upset, and I have no idea what's going on at the hotel. This is more than a fire to put out, because I lit the damn thing.

"But doesn't this change things?"

Kase lifts his brows. "It doesn't change anything. I still want you here. I don't care if Edwin has to sleep in the barn."

I stare down into my cup, remembering last night's conversation and my promise to stay. I'm nowhere close to being ready to leave Kase, but giving in to his plea in the throes of passion doesn't resolve anything in my heart when it comes to the land. I could go home and try to fix this seemingly unfixable situation. But maybe the extra time here at the farm will give me a chance to figure out a better way to appease my father and save Kase's family's legacy.

He tips my chin up, his eyes searching mine. "What's on your mind?"

I shrug. *What* isn't *on my mind?*

"What do you want to do? Anything you want. I'm all yours," he presses.

He smirks, and my heart skips a beat. When my thoughts drift to last night, I'm tempted to suggest we go straight back to bed. But no matter how obsessed I am with the physical highs of being with him, no amount of time between the sheets will guarantee us forever. And forever is fast what I'm starting to want with Kase.

"If you really want me to stay..." I hook my finger into the top of his belt buckle. "How about you show me the rest of the farm?"

He hesitates. "Are you sure? We could go out—"

"Show me your home, Kase." I glance up. "Let me see this place the way you do."

He crosses his arms and looks me up and down, from my bare toes to my frayed jean shorts and simple T-shirt. "All right, June. If that's what you want, that's what we'll do. You'd better put your boots on, though. Things can get dirty around here."

CHAPTER FIFTEEN

We pack a lunch and ourselves into Kase's truck. My thoughts are still swimming with questions about what went down between my father and Edwin, but I allow my curiosity about Kase's world to take up the foreground.

We don't have to travel far to find the pasture, where dozens of cows roam. We hop out of the truck, and Kase ventures ahead, his stride confident. The silhouette of his body appears strong and at ease.

We near the fence, and he casts his gaze out ahead of us.

"This is the heart of it. The reason I'm up at the crack of dawn every day instead of sleeping in with you."

He winks, and I smile because I've yet to wake up in his arms. As much as I cherish his sweet notes, nothing measures up to his presence. Unable to keep from touching him simply because I can, I thread our fingers together.

A few heifers with pretty markings linger a few feet away. They lift their heads from their feast of grass and turn their big brown eyes toward us. Not a care in the world. Lucky beasts.

I rest my head against Kase's shoulder with a sigh and watch them.

"They're cute. I've always thought so."

He chuckles. "They're all right. They don't smell great, which is why I'm not bothering to show you the barn."

In the distance, a calf prances near its mother. Dozens more adults huddle in groups across the field of green. "How many are there?"

"A hundred and fifteen. They get milked twice a day, every day. Even on holidays."

"Wow."

He's silent a moment. "It's hard work, and we're at the mercy of the market for what we're paid. Edwin's been doing it his whole life, and there were three generations before that."

I hesitate, not wanting to offend him with the question on my mind.

"Do you think it's sustainable?"

He shrugs. "Sure, over time. Have to be able to survive when times are tough, and not get too cocky when things are good. It's a matter of catching up now. When I left, Edwin had to hire more help to fill the void, and then prices tanked."

I stare out at the undeniably beautiful landscape. The financial pressures facing the farm are real, but not for lack of hard work. I wish I had some wisdom to offer, but I'm afraid I'm useless to Kase when it comes to advice. All I know is the hotel business, which couldn't be more different than their operation here.

"How are you going to make it work?"

I look up at him, wishing I saw more confidence in his posture.

He sighs. "Something has to change. But change is risky and expensive. If we take a chance on something new, it could fail and we'll be worse off than we are right now."

"Then why not sell? Why not give Edwin the retirement he'll need one day? Give yourself a chance to start fresh on something you'll really love."

"Look at all this." He gestures out to the pasture, the picturesque landscape of lush green rolling hills against a backdrop of cool blue mountains and sky. "This is the view I grew up with. Same as you. Except you take care of tourists and I take care of cows. It's a means to getting to stay in this beautiful place. Keeping the farmhouse and all the memories in it. There's no halfway with what your father wants. It's all or nothing, and as many problems as it would solve, selling means saying goodbye to everything I've known here. Forever. It's a big decision."

I can't argue with him, because I've seen the plans to transform the nine hundred acres of property, farmland, and buildings into something dramatically different. Rows of luxury townhomes and overflow vacation rentals that would supplement accommodations at the hotel. Nothing about that plan is compatible with the farm as it stands now.

As my heart begins to sink, Kase kisses the top of my head. "Come on. There's a lot more to see," he says, quiet understanding in his eyes.

With no more talk of the business of the farm, we get back in Kase's truck and drive the perimeter of the property for a while. He points out the different fields where they grow and harvest alfalfa and various crops to feed the farm's livestock. The property is as vast as the hotel's. Where ours is manicured, his is functional, every part of it meant to support the dairy operation or supplement their income. Both have their hidden treasures, though.

He points out the apple orchard from a distance, which brings back some vivid memories, but he doesn't stop until we reach the edge of a field tall with wheat. We park near an enormous red combine, and I follow Kase toward it.

"Am I about to get a lesson in harvesting?"

"I figure while you're here, might as well give you a ride and get some work done too." He bounces his keys in his hands, mischief in his eyes. Opening the door, he turns back to help me into the cab. "Hop up."

Using his firm grip as leverage, I hoist myself up, but there's only one seat. Before I can point this out, Kase settles me on his lap. I have no idea where to begin but trust that Kase knows what he's doing.

"Are you sure about this?"

He turns his keys in the ignition. "Hell yeah." After adjusting a few settings, we're set in motion. Not fast, not slow. Just the right speed to cut the wheat with minimal waste, he assures me. His focus is trained on the settings and what's ahead. Then he places my hands on the wheel, covering them with the soft, reassuring weight of his.

"What do I do?"

He points ahead. "Turn up here at the end of the field, and we'll lap back."

The combine is enormous compared to anything I've ever driven, but Kase is calm and steady, guiding my turns. We take a few more rounds up and down the field. The journey is almost calming once my nervousness settles, and I'm more comfortable with the wheel. Kase's warmth at my back and encouragement in my ear is a constant reassurance.

"I think we might turn you into a farmer yet," he says.

I smile. "This is actually pretty fun. I could see myself doing this."

He laughs softly. "Probably my favorite part of the job. Of course, it's a lot more fun with you in my lap."

He skims his hands down the sides of my ribs, digging in just enough to make me squirm. I swat him away.

"Hey, hands on the wheel." He nuzzles my hair. "This is serious business."

"You're just trying to cop a feel."

He hums, settling his hands on my hips. "Last pass. Then it's time for lunch. I know just the place."

Anticipation lights up in my belly as we park the combine and return to the truck. I don't have to ask where he's taking us next, because a couple minutes later, he's driving us over uneven landscape toward the orchard. We go over a bump, and it scoots me to the space right next to him.

He lets his foot off the gas and looks over at me. "You okay?"

I giggle and loop my arm into his. "I'm fine. It's not even raining."

He laughs and gives my thigh a squeeze. "Wouldn't want that ruining our picnic, would we?"

I bite my lip, because I have a feeling he's thinking about where we left off yesterday.

We park and go to the same spot. I lay out the blanket and kneel down to unpack our lunch. If I don't occupy myself with that task, I'm not sure if I'll be able to keep my hands off Kase. When he sits beside me, I half expect him to toss me onto my back and ravage me. But he surprises me by taking the sandwich I made and tearing into it with a hearty bite.

"Hungry much?"

He swallows and reaches for a water bottle in the basket. "You wore me out last night. I need protein."

I shove at his arm. "You were the one on a mission."

He lifts an eyebrow. "Says the woman who nearly broke skin begging me to fuck her harder when I was three steps from the bedroom."

My face heats. Embarrassment prickles under my skin. God, I really was a woman possessed last night. I'm not sure I could have stopped myself, but maybe it was too much.

"I'm sorry."

He takes another bite, his eyes sparkling with humor. "Are you seriously apologizing?"

"Did I leave marks?"

He takes a swig of water, a smirk curling his lips. "Probably. Won't be the last time, hopefully. I might leave a mark or two on you someday too. You going to forgive me?"

My cheeks flush even warmer. I think he knows the answer to that already, so I focus on the sandwich in my lap and begin to eat. A few empty minutes pass.

I finish my sandwich and pick up a container of strawberries I'd packed. The fresh fruit is soft and ripe on my tongue. I make a small sound of appreciation and offer one to Kase.

"Try these strawberries. I picked them up at the farm stand down the road the other day."

He looks down and then into my eyes. "Feed it to me."

I hesitate a second before bringing it to his mouth. Never

breaking eye contact, he consumes the red berry. As I pull away, he grabs my hand and sucks the end of my fingertip as if he missed something. The sensuous lash of his tongue, the velvet texture along the pad of my finger, does something to my insides.

"Delicious. Give me another one," he says, releasing me.

"You should grow some," I say.

I wince, realizing the stupidity of what I've said. God, I'm so mixed up. One minute I'm expecting Edwin and my father to sign on the dotted line to make this damn sale happen. The next, I'm falling in love with Kase and his dreams.

"Maybe I will." His calm reply draws my attention back to him.

Not wanting to let him on to my inner turmoil, I bring another berry to his mouth. He takes it between his teeth, and something about the look in his eyes compels me to let my fingertips linger on his lips. He chews, and the second his lips open, I push in, seeking more decadent swipes of his tongue. He takes my hand again, holding me there so he can suck and lick and nip for a long moment.

Everything about it reminds me of his mouth on other parts of me. I'm fixated, at the mercy of his every move, waiting for his next command...

CHAPTER SIXTEEN

We only get through one more strawberry before I'm on my back. I'm relieved and frustrated at once. Kase takes his time stripping away my clothes, from my boots to my bra, the only undergarment I permitted myself to wear since his banishment of panties.

He lies beside me, still clothed, ravaging me with his hot stare.

"Goddamn. If I'd known how perfect you were under clothes, June, there's no way I could have kept my hands off you that long."

"Well...these two weeks are about making up for lost time, aren't they?" I twirl a strand of my hair around my finger and tug at my bottom lip, hoping he takes the bait. His admiration warms me from the inside out, but I want a whole lot more.

"Damn right, they are," he mutters as he lowers his mouth to mine, consuming my next breath with a heated kiss.

My fingers tangle in his hair. I open my thighs, waiting to have his weight and strength powering between them. My God, I had no idea a man could make me this crazy, this hungry for contact.

Breaking away, he kisses the corner of my mouth, my chin, my collarbone, until he hovers at my breasts. With painstaking restraint, he draws slow circles with his tongue around my nipple. When I arch, he grasps my breast tightly and sucks the taut bud deep into his mouth.

"Oh!" I press my legs together against the rush of sensation I'm experiencing there too.

"Told you I was going to tease you, June," he says as he continues licking and sucking, teasing and tantalizing me at a pace that is nowhere near matching my need.

When he finally pulls away, I wait not so patiently for him to undress and finally take me. I ache for his savage thrusts. His erotic groans in my ear as he plunders my body and takes me to breathtaking heights.

Instead, he reaches over, takes the last strawberry, and rests it on my lips.

"Eat," he commands gently.

I open and accept the offering. He watches me chew, and then, as I did, pushes his fingers past my lips.

I swirl around his two fingers, sucking the salt off with the juice on my tongue. He watches intently, his lips falling open, his groin growing hard against my thigh.

"I want to disappear inside you, June. Between these luscious lips." He slides in and out, then again, before drawing a damp trail down my chin, between my breasts, and over my belly until he's between my thighs. He nudges my legs wide and sinks two fingers deep into my heat. "And these."

I release a contented sigh. Then he grazes the same place that sent me into orbit last night. I shudder and suck in a sharp breath.

"You remember me here?"

"It's so intense," I whimper, clenching around him.

He massages the same place at the top of my inner wall, over and over, gently but with increasing pressure. I buck my hips, already feeling wildly out of control of my body's responses. Every pulse is like an electric shock too powerful to ignore.

He sweeps in and presses a full kiss to my lips as he twists his fingers inside me. "No one's going to know your body's secrets like I will, June," he rasps. "I'm already so addicted to you. You know that, right? The way you taste. The way you smell. Every fucking curve calls me. The way you give in and take all of me... You do more than take it. You want it like you can't possibly live without it. And when you do, June, you turn all this hurt into something I can live with. How am I supposed to ever let you go?"

I stare up at him with heart-wrenching awe. "You never have to. I'm right here."

I'm never leaving.

He kisses me again, sealing my silent proclamation in the hot melding of our mouths.

"You're here, baby, and you're so ripe for the things I want to do to you. Like those sweet berries, I just want to take a bite and feel you give. Feel you bend and break before you explode on my tongue."

I close my eyes with a breathy sigh. His words are poetry written on my body, inked into my psyche, carved into new desires I never knew I possessed.

"You trust me?"

His words are made of smooth stone, heavy and confident. He already knows.

I open my eyes to him and lift my chin. He pulls back and rolls me onto my belly. Positioning my wrists at the small of my back, he binds them with some kind of fabric. His motions are slow but firm, all the more tantalizing when I can't see him. Then he hoists my hips up so I'm on my knees. The side of my face is pressed into the blanket, the mane of my ponytail splayed over my shoulder. He'd had me in a similar position here before, but with my arms bound I'm even more vulnerable.

He rises behind me, just out of view. I hear the clank of metal and the dull huff of clothes hitting the ground. The seconds feel like minutes. Panic and anxiety flutter in my belly when I think about us being caught. The moments are fleeting though and only seem to intensify the desire raging in my core. The places where he's already touched and teased are buzzing.

I hear him settle behind me and relish the way his rough naked thighs and calves bracket mine. He draws his palms down my arms and slows over my bared ass.

"You want me to mark you, June?"

Dark desire laces his offer. Goosebumps race over my skin.

I draw in a shaky breath and exhale, reaching for a person who only exists inside these moments with Kase.

"Yes... Spank me, please."

A few seconds pass with only the sound of Kase's breath.

"You're a fast learner," he says before landing a hard slap on my ass.

I bite my lip to keep from making a sound. One lash of his palm turns into more. I accept them with a series of grunts and moans. I dig my toes into the blanket but otherwise barely move. Inward, I channel the spike of my senses, discomfort, and turmoil of emotions. I use all of it to feed the storm, until the searing heat of my flesh matches the raging fire inside.

When he stops, I'm breathless. A fine sheen of sweat covers

my skin. I'm edgy, existing in some subspace between pain and uncontrollable lust, equal parts unfulfilled and blissed out from the endorphins blazing through my system.

He grasps my wrists firmly, and I feel the head of his cock pressed to my opening.

"So wet. So perfect."

Instinct drives me to push back against him, and he allows me to gain a bare inch of his penetration.

"Go ahead. Show my cock how much you liked that."

I rock back a little more, again and again until I think he's filling me. I realize how much I've fallen short when he meets my little pushes with a powerful thrust of his own, rooting himself so deeply I suck in a sharp breath and exhale a throaty moan.

He doesn't wait for me to acclimate to him or ease me to his rhythm. His next drives are hard and merciless. A jarring cocktail of pleasure pain not unlike his spanking. In this position, I feel overfull. It's too much of everything. The pleasure and the pain. And I'm powerless to ease the pressure or control where it's heading.

"Kase." My voice trembles with uncertainty. "I can't—"

He gives my wrists a tug and winds the tail of my hair around his hand, using both as leverage to pull me upright. Letting go of my wrists, he bands his arm around my ribcage, holding my back to his front.

"You need to trust me, June," he says against my ear.

"I do. It's just so deep."

He drives his hips up slowly, pulling my body down so the tip of his cock seems to kiss some new place inside.

"Let go," he whispers, kissing my neck.

"I—" *I want to...*

"I'll help you."

With that softly worded promise, he brings his fingers to my mouth. "Suck. Make them wet."

I do as he asks, moaning as he plunges his fingers and his cock into me in sync.

Then he drifts lower, lubricating my clit with my own juices.

"Kase... Oh God." I tremble under his touch. Any restraint my body held falls away like the last wisp of a dandelion.

"You're perfect. The way you move. The way you submit."

My eyes roll back when he punches his hips up. Simultaneously, he folds his fingers into my ponytail, gripping my hair tightly. The sting counters the delirious wave of pleasure of his cock and fingers working in and over me. My brain doesn't know which sensation to land on. My body sings and soars under the harmony of everything at once—a concert of sensual awareness orchestrated by Kase. The master of my pleasure, the king of my heart.

I love this. I love him...

I'm his. His plaything, his lover, his to command. His to take...

As he powers into me, restrains me, and guides me to the precipice of a brand of pleasure I've never known, I can feel the words form on my lips. I want so badly to tell him how I feel now, but I need to see his eyes. Need to see his answer and hold it in my heart. Need to know if he feels the same way...

"Kase..."

I'm ready to beg him to turn me around or just scream that I love him into the pure country air, when he stops me with his next command.

"You're going to come for me, June," he says roughly. "You're going to fucking break wide open for me. I want to hear it on your lips. I want to taste it in your sweat. Come on my cock. Come apart, baby."

"Yes... Yes..."

I'm shaking, weak and coiled up too tight, trapped in his dominating pace. Then I'm there, exactly where he wants me, ready to fall apart.

The orgasm is like a glowing pearl just out of reach. Drawn into my body on my next desperate breath. Drifting lower, pulsing around my heart, filling my chest. He sinks his teeth into my shoulder, and the pearl detonates. Deep in my core, down every limb. All around his punishing thrusts.

My scream turns into a choking sob as I collapse against his chest, utterly wasted.

He unties my binds, lays my limp body on the blanket, and rolls me to face him. He simply stares at me for a few breathless seconds.

"You're so beautiful. My God, June."

Tension lines his face and shoulders. His cock is still rigid and jutting out from his gorgeous body. I sober a little to think that after my explosive, toe-curling fireworks of an orgasm, I'd left him unsatisfied. Not fair. Not fair at all.

"Did you already...?"

He shakes his head. "Amazingly, no."

I reach for him and pull him down over me. "I want you to," I murmur.

"I will." He reaches between us and fills me slowly. "Over and over. For as long as you'll have me."

My heart skips a beat at the tender look in his eyes, their beauty rivaling the endless sky stretching all around us. The feeling is more than a pang in my heart. It's everywhere. In my pores. Humming under my skin. All-consuming warmth and truth. It's so big and so undeniable that it finally spills from my thoughts...

"Kase... I love you."

I speak the words from the depth of my heart, no longer afraid.

He closes his eyes, opening them a second later. He brushes his thumb across my lips. Then, with a searing kiss, he begins making love to me. In the silence, we climb together. I'm still sensitive. Still buzzing from limb to limb and completely committed to witnessing his pleasure.

My confession seems to echo between us. I lock my heels around his waist when another rocket ship climax fires through me. This time Kase follows me down, gasping for air, digging into my flesh and holding on to me like I might disappear and steal away this precious moment.

As he stills, our gazes lock.

"I love you, June Bell. I can't remember a time when I didn't want to." He touches my face, his expression soft. "Now, I'll never know a time when I don't."

My heart swells. I cup my hand along his stubbled jaw. "I like the sound of that. Very much."

CHAPTER SEVENTEEN

We spend another hour lying naked in the orchard, enjoying the afterglow of our lovemaking and newly minted confessions. Dressed and our picnic packed, we go back to the truck and drive back to the empty farmhouse.

We shower together. We don't speak much, but our touches are filled with meaning, delicate traces along the new places where our souls have been sewn together. There'll be no falling out of love with Kase McCasker, no matter what happens with the land.

We towel off and kiss and dress. We smile and tease and almost consider falling back into bed, when the back door squeaks open and slams shut. Edwin is home.

We go downstairs. As high as I am on Kase, I'm still worried about what's happened at the hotel.

Kase takes my hand, and we meet Edwin in the living room, where he's sitting on the couch, staring into nothing.

"Hey, how'd it go today?"

Edwin looks up, his features haggard from one more day stacked onto a lifetime of hard work. His gaze darts calmly between Kase and me. I feel naked and exposed, like he knows everything we've been up to since I got here. He has to know I've been in Kase's bed. He may even suspect we're already hopelessly in love with each other.

"Hi, Edwin," I say.

He nods. "June." He leans his head back on the couch. "Going fine out there. Just taking a rest before the second shift. Don't mind me."

Kase frowns. "I got it. June and I had all day. I'll finish things up out there."

Edwin shakes his head. "It's all right. I'm just a little tired. Didn't sleep great last night."

Suddenly, I feel like the houseguest who has no place. I can't help but register guilt when our eyes meet, and I know that has all to do with my father. Of course, if I hadn't been caught necking with Kase in his truck, Edwin might still be enjoying some time off at the hotel.

Kase leans down and laces up his boots before rising again. He turns to me. "I'll be back in a few hours, all right?"

I nod. "Sure. I'll work up something for dinner."

He smiles and gives me a chaste kiss. "Don't burn the house down."

I lightly punch his arm and he turns with a laugh, disappearing out the back door, taking my heart and his addictive warm glow with him. So this is love. Crazy, addictive, all-consuming love. No wonder people call it a drug. He's been out the door ten seconds, and I'm ready for another hit.

Edwin pushes up to his feet and walks toward the kitchen. "Want a beer?" he calls back over his shoulder.

I follow him. "No, thanks."

He opens the fridge, bends, and takes out a cold brew. I loosely consider our options for dinner, as if this is normal life. Me in the kitchen, killing time while Kase works, figuring out what to feed him so we can end the night tangled up with each other.

But Edwin's presence makes it harder to pretend. He's tired and visibly agitated.

"Hard day?"

He shrugs a shoulder. "My body doesn't like it, but I'm used to it." He sighs, resignation set in his features. "I figured out a couple years ago that I've got Lyme disease. No idea when I got it. With all the time I've spent in the woods, it could have been in my system for decades. In any case, it's slowing me down faster than I'd like."

"That's awful."

"I may be worn down, but I'd rather take orders from the cows than your father. I'll sleep when I die."

"I'm sorry," I say.

He takes a swig from his beer and leans back against the counter. "You don't have anything to be sorry about, June. Kase and I dragged you into this mess. If we hadn't, you'd be living in your castle none the wiser."

I contemplate the sentiment, but something about his tone and meaning riles me.

"I think you know better than most how much good comes from keeping people in the dark."

He slides his gaze toward me and drains his beer a little more. He swallows and exhales. "I guess Kase told you everything, then."

I nod. "He's still hurting. He's got this love-hate relationship with you and the farm. I don't regret him bringing me here, but I really wish I wasn't in the middle of all of it."

He shakes his head. "He's been mixed up about you and this

farm for as long as I can remember. Nothing new about that except he's taken you to bed, and I imagine that doesn't uncomplicate a damn thing."

I can feel myself blushing.

He doesn't seem to notice. He looks out the window and then down at the old pine floor and pinches his brows. "Hell, I can't even blame Ger for blowing a gasket. Feels like Juliette all over again. Nothing but a lifetime's worth of heartbreak and pain came from that. God, she's probably having a good laugh about it now."

I knit my brows together. "What does my mother have to do with anything?"

He lifts his gaze. His features seem frozen with realization. "June, tell me he told you about your mother."

I press a few short breaths out of my chest, making me dizzy and unstable.

He puts the bottle down on the counter and straightens. "You said he told you everything."

I swallow hard. "He told me about your sister, Lily. How she came home and left him with you to raise. About how he grew up believing you were his father until he left for school. He was devastated."

He lets out a hollow laugh. "He'd tell you that, of course. Unbelievable."

I brace one hand on the counter. "What isn't he telling me?"

He tenses his jaw and avoids my eyes. "I told you before, June. This isn't my story to tell."

"Then whose is it?" I can't hide the outrage in my voice, but in this moment, it seems like everyone's holding on to a truth that's evaded me.

"Your father's," he snaps. "Far be it for me to spoil the fairy tale he's been having you living in."

I take another step toward him, my patience wearing paper thin. "If it's about my mother, I need you to tell me. Tell me what Kase should have. Tell me everything my father's been holding back."

He paces the room, rubbing the back of his neck and muttering curses under his breath.

"Edwin, please."

Tears prickle my eyes.

He pauses.

"Edwin, all I've got is a painting of her that hangs in my father's office and a story about how she was taken from us too soon."

He closes his eyes. "What if she isn't who you thought she was?"

"The truth is better than nothing."

Isn't it?

He draws in a deep breath and exhales loudly. His posture is rigid, like a sudden fear grips him. He looks up at the ceiling. Nothing but yellowing paint there. He closes his eyes and exhales another tired sigh.

"June, I was in love with your mother."

I nod, because my suspicions from the picture already hinted as much.

"Not just a summer fling. Not puppy love. What we had... It was the kind of love that's so strong, so powerful, when it gets ripped away, you're never right again. Never whole." He pauses a moment. His eyes take on a faraway look. "The day she died, something died inside me too. Something I'll never get back. And I'll never forgive myself. If I hadn't loved her so damn much, if I could have just let her go, she'd still be here. She'd be with your father, but she'd be here. Living and breathing."

His eyes mist and mine do the same. His pain seems to fill the room, casting darker shadows on the grief I already feel from her absence. Edwin's pain is different, though. It's more like an aching regret. But accidents happen. Loving her or hating her wouldn't ever change the ice on the road that night.

"The accident wasn't your fault."

His features are pinched. "What did Ger tell you?"

"It happened on her way home from a night working at the hotel."

He shakes his head. "She worked that night, sure. I saw her after she finished up. We hadn't seen each other in a few months. She came here to talk. Kase was still little, asleep upstairs in his room. I wasn't going to try to win her back that night, but it was like everything that ever mattered between us came back full force. We couldn't keep our hands off each other. I made love to her. And when she had to go back home, I begged her to let me find a way for us to make it work. I'd made a good life for Kase and me here. I could do that for her and you too, if she'd only let me."

My jaw falls agape. "She was going to leave my dad?"

He shakes his head solemnly. "Never had the chance. We'd made some tearful promises. But she went back home that night. I wasn't expecting to hear from her so soon, but she called me a few hours later. Hysterical. Crying. Saying she was coming to stay with me for a couple days. Of course I said that was fine. I was upset for her, but God, for those couple hours I was so damn happy to know I was finally getting her back."

My next half breath fills my lungs painfully. Edwin's truth wraps around them like barbed wire.

"What happened?"

He pinches the bridge of his nose again. "Your grandparents' house was on the outskirts of town. The temperature had dropped, and the roads were icy. She lost control and collided with an oncoming car on a curve." His lip quivers. "It happened just how you probably heard it, June. Except she wasn't coming home to you. She was coming back to me."

Tears burn behind my eyes. I let go of the counter. My hands are shaking.

"Kase knew this?"

Edwin works his jaw. "Once he got older, after a few less-than-friendly encounters with your father, I told him what happened with Juliette. I hadn't told him about his mother yet, so in his mind, he thought she may have left because of what happened between Juliette and me. I didn't know he'd spin it that way, but I figured it didn't matter if it kept him away from you anyway."

I swallow hard, disbelief piling on to betrayal and resentment. In an instant, I run through a dozen memories of a younger Kase. His brooding stares. His almost touches. The energy that radiated off him that I could never pinpoint but was drawn to nonetheless. It all makes sense now.

"He looked at me sometimes like he hated me, or like he knew something I didn't. This was it. This was why."

"He doesn't hate you, June."

I can barely make Edwin out behind the haze of my impending

tears. When they spill over, I turn and rush up the stairs. I shut the door and then pace around Kase's bedroom.

Kase's bedroom.

This is where he slept every night, growing up believing I came from a woman who ruined his family. This is where I gave him something precious... Something I'd only ever wanted to give to him.

I repress a sob, only to push more tears down my cheeks. How could he keep this from me?

And why?

A fresh wave of devastation knocks me to my knees. I take fistfuls of the quilt and bury my face in the softness, shaking my head against the next thought plaguing me.

What if this deal is simply a ruse to exact revenge? To act on the resentment he carried for so long? What if nothing I think we have is real?

I cry for what seems like forever. Long, painful sobs that tear fresh wounds everywhere I'd stitched dreams of our future together. His breathless "I love yous" are painful brands on my heart that may never heal. Our memories together, so fresh in my mind, already hurt like hell.

I lift my head and look out the window. The amber sky hints at dusk nearing. I can't face him. I can't hear him lie or apologize to try to keep me here again.

I rise slowly and wipe my face. I toss my laundry and toiletries in my suitcase, hardly caring if I leave anything behind.

Another tear rolls down to my chin and drops to the floor. I'm saying goodbye to Kase... To a home I never thought I'd have grown so fond of.

I spot a small notepad on top of Kase's dresser. I pick it up, rip a page off, and grab a nearby pen. I hover the tip above the page, my hand trembling.

More tears fall.

No words come.

CHAPTER EIGHTEEN

I drive for a couple hours. Down back roads. Along the rivers and roads that cut between the mountains. I drive until my fear is gone. Until the pain dulls a little. Until the chaos in my mind quiets enough for me to face my father with what I know now.

Everything still hurts. I'm angry and lost, but none of that changes what's happened. Nothing brings my mother back. Nothing can take back my father's lies or Kase's omissions.

I pull into the hotel lot and drag my suitcase to the front porch. Marty greets me, though his chipper smile fades when he sees me up close.

"Miss Bell. Are you all right?"

"I'm fine. Could you please have my bag taken up to my room?"

"Of course. Right away."

He takes the suitcase from me and turns to go inside, but I stop him.

"Do you know where my father is?"

"I think he's in the dining hall." A frown mars his brow. "Are you sure you're all right?"

I touch his shoulder as I pass. "Thank you, Marty. I'll be fine."

I will be. I'll have to be. My life can't end over a broken heart.

I go inside and head to the dining hall, trying to avoid making eye contact with any of the guests. I can't imagine how I must look. I hear my father's voice echoing in the big room. I have no idea what day it is or what's on the hotel's agenda, but he's likely trying to coordinate a special event at this hour.

He's talking with Helene, our catering director, as I approach. I'm several feet away when he turns. His face falls when he sees me.

"June." He glances back to Helene. "I'll be right back."

We meet in the middle. "Junebug. Are you okay? What's happened? Did he hurt you?"

I shake my head and open my lips to speak, but the well of emotion is overflowing again that quickly. He hushes me quietly and leads me out of the hall. We duck into his office, and he closes the door behind us.

"Sit down. Talk to me, June."

I take a seat in one of the old red velvet chairs on the other side of his desk, and he takes the other. In those few seconds of silence, I'm grateful for this room. Edwin may hate our castle. It may not be *a* home. But it's still my home. It's familiar, and right now that's what I need. Something steady. Something true...

I reach into my back pocket and pull out the photograph. I run my finger over the four faces looking back at me. "Edwin told me what happened. It makes sense now why you always hated him."

He takes the photo from me. His lips are tight. "This is old. Before you were born. Where'd you find it?"

"The suitcase in your closet. How come you didn't tell me the truth, Daddy? Why did I have to find out from a stranger?"

He stands, tosses the photo on the desk, and paces slowly around the room. His gaze is cast down, his hands tucked into his slacks.

"I have no excuses to give you," he says, sadness lacing his tone. "I loved your mother. I don't love her any less because she was leaving me the night she died. I don't ever want you to think that."

When our eyes meet, I know he's telling me the truth. His shoulders sag in resignation. He's got the same kind of regret painted on his features as Edwin did. My heart breaks for all of us. For the tragedy they lived and we all suffered for.

"What happened? Will you tell me now?"

He pauses a moment. "Edwin stole her away from me the same way I stole her away from him. All's fair in love and war, right?" He nods to the photo. "They were together first. The other woman was only in Falls Edge for a summer. We had fun, but Juliette was in my eye. Except there was no getting between her and Edwin. They were infatuated."

He looks up at the painting of my mother, her regal smile looking down on both of us. "I'd like to tell you that ours was true love and theirs wasn't, but I'd probably be wrong. When Edwin's sister came into town, baby in tow, everything changed. Juliette thought Edwin was crazy to take on a child that wasn't his own. As much as he loved her, he couldn't abandon the boy. Juliette... She was..."

He turns, drops into his chair, and pulls a bottle of scotch from his drawer. After filling and draining the glass, he sits back.

"Juliette came from a good family. They had money. You know that. They bought the hotel and knew what kind of experience the patrons wanted. Juliette, being their only child, grew up expecting life to go a certain way. Girl meets boy. Big white wedding. Baby. Happily ever after."

"And Kase didn't fit in with that picture."

"It was bad enough Edwin came from a farming family. Taking on someone else's child was too much. She couldn't help feeling like he'd chosen Kase over her, over their relationship. They argued over it and split up for a little while to think things through. That's when I took my chance. I pursued her. Ruthlessly. I was determined to give her everything Edwin couldn't. I'd been to college. Came from a good family. I could help her run the hotel. Not to mention I was head over heels in love with her. I'd give her the world."

"Then you married her."

"First chance I could. Everything moved fast. I told myself it was because I was finally the one to make her dreams come true. The missing puzzle piece. But deep down I knew she was running from Edwin. Running hard and fast away from the life she couldn't have with him. We got married, and in the blink of an eye, she was pregnant with you. Everyone was thrilled. Her parents were happy. She was happy. Glowing. Everything was perfect for a while. But after you were born and she went back to work at the hotel, things started to change."

"Change how?"

He shrugs. "Sometimes things just change. Maybe she was tired. Maybe she was overwhelmed. I have no idea why she went to see Edwin that night. All I know is when she came home and told me she was leaving me, I thought someone had cut out my heart. I wasn't going to let her go. I couldn't lose her." He pauses for a long moment. "June, I did something I will always regret. Something you'll probably never forgive me for." Tears glimmer in his eyes. "I struck her."

I steel my jaw and fight to hold back my anger.

"I didn't know what else to do. I felt so powerless. I felt like there was no stopping her. I was losing her. To *him*. And if I lost her, it meant I could lose you too. He'd raise you. They'd make their family out of you and Kase, and..." He rubs at his eyes, wiping away the wetness. "I couldn't stop her. I just couldn't stop her..."

Several minutes pass. More tears fall between the two of us. All the while, my mother looks down on us, her smile almost mocking in the face of our grief.

"I wish you had told me, Daddy."

He exhales a shaky sigh. "When she died, I put it all away. Buried it so deep, June. I never wanted to think about any of it again. I just wanted to throw myself into running the hotel and being the best father I knew how to be. And you always seemed too young for the whole truth, so I kept avoiding it."

I stare at the floor. I'm exhausted. Wrung out and wrung out again. With all the emotions pinging around, what I expect the least is a measure of relief. But with the truth now out, once and for all, I'm awash with it. For that, I'm grateful. Almost at peace. Almost...

"I'm going up to bed now. Thank you for telling me," I say quietly.

He watches me rise and go to the door. "What happened with Kase, June?"

I slow at the door, rest my hand on the old metal knob. "I left. That's what happened."

A moment passes.

"So what do we do now?"

I look over my shoulder. "I don't know, Daddy. I really don't know."

★ ★ ★ ★

I wake late the next morning. My head throbs from all the crying I did. My heart aches when I relive the whole emotional roller-coaster of the day. The truth hurts, but I'd relive the pain over and over to find my way out of the dark again. I deserved to know more, and now, finally, I do.

A pang of regret hits me when I think of Kase. I probably shouldn't have left so hastily. I should have at least left a note, though I still don't know what I would have said. He of all people should know what it's like to have the world upended that way. To have believed a lie for so long. To feel betrayed and underestimated by the ones who fed you that lie.

It's not my story to tell.

Edwin's words chime through my mind as I meander downstairs to the lobby. Perhaps he had a point. Perhaps the onus of retelling the circumstances around my mother's death should have fallen on my father's shoulders only. Whether or not our love and every intimate and emotionally charged moment between us was as real as I pray it was, perhaps expecting Kase to break the truth wide open to me in my short time at the farmhouse was not entirely fair.

Doesn't dull the hurt. Doesn't undo what's done. But I'm closer to being ready to face him again, knowing all that I do.

The lobby is fairly quiet. It's afternoon already, and most of the guests are on the grounds or out doing touristy things in town. Not seeing my father, I venture out onto the veranda. Julie is behind the bar, moving with efficiency to fill a drink order. When I approach, she pauses and lights up.

"June! Where the hell have you been? Your dad said you were taking some time off. I miss your face, girl."

I manage a smile. The familiarity of the hotel is starting to unpack some of my malaise.

"I was," I say, having no desire to elaborate. "Do you have the schedule back there? I want to grab some shifts this week."

"Sure." She disappears and pops back up with a binder.

I take it and look for open slots while Julie prattles on about Mackie's and the new stranger in town who's got her all twisted up in the very best way.

I'm wrapped up in my own drama, but hearing about hers is surprisingly cathartic. I pencil myself in for a few shifts and give her the schedule back. For the first time in a long time, I'm eager to get back to work, not for the sake of the hotel and lending a helping hand, but because I need an occupation to ground me in the wake of everything that's happened. And if serving Old Fashioneds to women in white pearls is all I've got, I'll gladly take it.

I say goodbye to Julie and pass by the reception area on my way to my father's office.

"June."

I halt when Martha, our most senior employee, gets my attention from behind the reception desk.

"Yes?"

"I have a note for you." She shuffles around her desk. "Oh, where is it?" A few seconds later she produces a folded letter and slides it over the counter. "Kase McCasker came by this morning. He wanted to see you. In fact, he was pretty adamant about it, but your father said no one was to disturb you this morning. He went to go speak to Mr. Bell himself." She grimaces slightly. "I don't know what was said, of course, but Mr. McCasker told me to give this to you before he left."

I grab the letter and walk away with it before she can say more. I hold it to my chest and find a quiet hallway. Tears spring from my eyes nearly the moment I unfold it. Kase's script is jagged, like he was angry when he wrote it. The words are few.

No matter what happens, I will never stop loving you.

Does yesterday have to change all the moments between us? Does the truth about the past have to change our future? I drag in an uneven breath and reread the line over and over again. I want to believe it. Every cell of my being wants to believe our love is true and nothing's changed between us.

I fold the note and put it in my pocket. Brushing away the tears, I go to my father's office. I'm relieved to find him there but unsettled that he appears so calm. My world is in tatters, and he's back to work as if nothing has changed. Maybe for him, nothing has. He's always known...

He looks up, his expression morphing from surprised to solemn.

"June." His eyes evade mine, furthering my unease. "How are you feeling?"

"What happened?" I skip right past the niceties. I'm tired and heartbroken and confused, and he knows it. "What did Kase say? Why didn't you let me see him?"

My voice is froggy, heavy with the heartache I feel. There's no use pretending Kase doesn't have the effect on me that he does. I'm in love with him. Hopelessly.

"He wanted to see you. I didn't think you needed to be bothered with anything this morning."

I drop into the seat across from his desk and stare until he looks up with a guilty look in his eyes.

"You're still trying to come between us, aren't you? You won't let this rift with the McCaskers go. Even now."

He shakes his head slightly. "That's not it. I just don't want to see you get hurt. I'm sorry, but the father in me figured you needed at least a day to process everything that happened yesterday. I had no idea what interactions you had with him, but I figured if it was upsetting enough to make you pack up and come home, he could wait."

I only half believe him.

"I was happy there, you know." I brush away another errant tear that slips down my cheek. "Until you showed up all angry, until you sent Edwin back home and he turned my world upside down, I was happy. With Kase, at the farm, just being with him. It was simple, and it felt like home in a way I've never experienced before. Don't you dare try to take it away from me again."

He's silent a moment, his lips pressed tight. "Fine, June. I won't. But the deal is done now. You need to accept that."

I wince. "No. It's not. I came back. That means it's off."

He pauses like he's bracing himself for my outrage.

"When Kase came in here asking for you, naturally, I asked him what he wanted to do about that land."

Seconds tick by. My stomach locks into a tight ball in anticipation of what's coming. "And what did he say?"

"I didn't pressure him one way or the other, June. He was angry, I could tell, but he stated in very clear terms that the deal was to be done. I spoke with my attorney this morning, and we'll be ready to close next week or sooner. As soon as the investor funds clear, this can all be over. I've let Edwin know, and honestly, I think he's looking forward to this being all said and done too."

I shake my head viciously. "Daddy, no. You can't do this. You can't just destroy it all."

"They've seen the plans. They know what the development will entail. They've had plenty of time to come to terms with it. There's no halfway on this."

I stand up. "But you don't understand because you've never spent time there. There are things worth saving. Hidden treasures."

"Like what?" He throws up his hands, like he can't possibly imagine there being an acre of the McCasker farm worth saving.

"Like... Like the orchard. And the pasture is beautiful. The views are incredible. They rival some of ours. And the farmhouse. It's small and needs a remodel, but Kase and his family have lived there for five generations. You can't just tear it down without a second thought."

He clenches his fists but speaks calmly and slowly. "June, this is not the time to get sentimental. All right? The McCaskers have made their choice now. There's been a lot of time and money put into all this planning. Architects and engineers. Legal fees, damn it. Why do you think I was so furious when it all fell through? It came out of my pocket, not theirs."

"That's not why. You wanted to erase the McCasker name from this town."

He's silent, and in that space I know what I've said is true.

"You've kept this hatred alive too long. You all have," I say.

"Maybe I have, but the farm is in financial trouble. Did they tell you that when they were touring you around the Garden of Eden down there?"

"Yes, they did, and something needs to change. I get it. But this plan..." I stamp my finger in the middle of one of the blueprints scattered across his mahogany desk. "*This* plan isn't the answer."

"Hell." He mutters the curse under his breath. He sinks back into his chair and tosses his pen on his desk. "That boy is smarter than I gave him credit for."

I blink rapidly. "What does that mean?"

"If all this were up to you, June... If you had the final say in it, you wouldn't let this sale happen, would you?"

"No," I say firmly. "Not the way you have it now."

His lips wrinkle into a frustrated grimace. "Great."

"What? What aren't you telling me?"

He sighs and runs his palms down his face. He's beginning to look as worn out as I feel. Finally.

"Daddy, what's going on?"

"Before you left to stay at the farm, Kase came to me and we talked about his proposal. He had a few conditions. You were to stay at the farm, uninterrupted, for two weeks. Edwin was to stay here, under the auspice of a vacation that could maybe turn into semiretired employment. And the third condition was that if and when the sale came about, there would be three required signatures on the purchase and sale. Edwin's. Mine. And yours."

"Mine? But I wouldn't be an owner. Nothing's in my name as it is."

"For this, you would be. He wanted your name on the deed. He reminded me of that condition this morning, in no uncertain terms."

Silence settles between us, feeding my spinning thoughts and highlighting my father's obvious disappointment. He looks down at the blueprints with a tired sigh.

"Like I said, he's a lot smarter than I gave him credit for."

CHAPTER NINETEEN

KASE

Four months later...

Sometimes a soul needs time to breathe. To convalesce. To crawl around in the dark until it finds some light.

June would have never left Falls Edge. Leaving me and the farmhouse couldn't have been easy, either. I saw the tear-stained paper she left. The note she couldn't write. Edwin told me about her wracking sobs. The agony in her eyes when he told her the truth.

I wasn't planning to stay away long. A week or so to give her space. She deserved that much.

Didn't matter that every minute without her made me sick. Didn't matter that my future looked like a black path paved to hell without her. Didn't matter, because I knew how she felt. I knew better than anyone how a blow like that could crumble all the walls around a person. Crack the very foundation under a person's feet. And then rain misery and pain down like a never-ending storm.

I could have told her about her mother and Edwin. I could have confessed that I'd been drawn to her before I made up my own version of the truth about Juliette chasing away my mother and wrecking my family. I could have explained how I followed her up the falls that night in pure defiance of the line drawn between us by the people who'd raised us. Because in a town as small as Falls Edge, you know pretty quickly who has the goods to break your heart. June Bell was always the one who did it for me. Smart. Beautiful. Forbidden...

She was all those things, and for a few precious days, she was mine too.

I could have told her everything, and I would have. One day, when I wasn't bleeding out with the love I had for her. When I wasn't fucking drowning in the indisputable truth that June Bell owned me. If I'd suspected it before, I knew it now. She held the power to make every dream I'd ever had come true.

And in my utter selfishness, I convinced myself that I deserved all of that more than she deserved the truth. I gambled it all on the chance at her heart. I manipulated the hell out of her and Edwin and her father, which, at the time, I figured was better than letting everyone keep hating each other for no other outcome than more hate and hurt. I never considered the hole in my heart she could leave me with.

I went up to the hotel the next day ready to fight for her, but June was as good as a princess locked in her tower. She didn't want to see me, Gerald said. She needed to process everything that had happened. I wanted to pummel the man and tear through every room in the hotel until I found her and could beg her for a chance to make things right. But even through my anger, I understood that she deserved time to heal. A chance to forgive.

But what then? What if she healed and never wanted to speak to me again? What if she decided to take back the love she gave to me so freely and give it to someone else, someone more deserving of her heart?

So I left. To give her space. To protect myself. I wasn't going to hang around Falls Edge to witness the utter ruin of my heart. I was barely living when she came back into my life as it was.

I'm not a better person for the distance. I'm still sick over her. She haunts my dreams. I curse the day I let myself believe I could be the one to change the course of our family, win the girl, and carve out a life at the farm. Everything about those broken dreams still hurts like hell.

A couple weeks turned into four months. I went back to my part-time gig tending bar near the university. I crashed with old buddies, believing it was all temporary. Until I woke up one morning hating myself for all the alcohol I'd consumed after a long shift, and realized this was becoming my life. My silence and self-imposed exile wasn't getting me any closer to a dream. No closer to getting over June. No closer to moving on.

All that's about to change.

★ ★ ★ ★

I scale the steps of the Falls Edge Hotel. It's fall and the veranda's closed, but I can't ignore a vision of June there with a tray in her hand, hair up in a ponytail that's never totally right, apron slung around her hips, and sunshine in her smile. And her eyes, those stormy green eyes that always made me want to press her against the wall and do things to her...

I blow out a frustrated breath and head for the reception desk.

"Hi there," I say.

Martha, the older woman at the front desk of the Falls Edge Hotel, blinks up at me. Last time I saw her, I could barely hold a pen to tell June that I loved her. That I always would. And I always would...

"Kase McCasker. Good seeing you. How can I help you today?"

"I was wondering if June was around."

She shakes her head. "Afraid not." Every line in her face communicates genuine disappointment.

She has no idea how hard and fast my heart is already plummeting.

"I can give her a message if you'd like," she says, new light in her eyes.

I hesitate. This is déjà vu all over again. "No, thanks."

I turn on my heel and walk toward the door.

"Kase, wait a minute."

I halt and look over my shoulder.

"If you were wanting to see her, you could head over to the farm. She's been overseeing the new development there."

I swallow hard and nod. "Thanks, Martha."

She smiles and waves as I disappear through the door. I jump into my truck and head for the farmhouse. Anxious, I drum my fingers on the steering wheel, trying not to feel miserable about the transformations that have taken place since I left. As soon as I heard the words "new development" pass Martha's lips, I knew June had signed off on it. I feel like a damn fool for holding on to some hope that she wouldn't jump at the chance, that her time at the farm had changed her heart.

Truth is I would have burned the damn house down to have her.

Instead I put Falls Edge in my rearview without the girl, and I left my dream for the future in the smug hands of her father. Salt on the wound, and it hurts now more than ever.

Gripping the steering wheel tighter, I catch sight of the farm up ahead. I brace myself, already regretting this whole thing. I should have picked a better way to move on. Reconnecting with June is like pulling on a thread that's been unraveling my life for years. What good can possibly come from it?

But when I roll up, it's as if nothing has changed. Edwin's truck is parked in the drive. The farmhouse is still there. The wood siding has been whitewashed. Fresh mulch lines the lily plants along the path up to the front porch, which is littered with construction materials. Half a dozen cabinet doors are lined up on saw horses, and every variety of sander is plugged in to a power strip that snakes back into the house through the front door.

I climb the stairs just as Edwin swings open the door, another cabinet door in hand. He tosses it down and pulls me into a tight hug.

"Kase! My God, son. Where the hell have you been?"

I close my eyes and hug him back. I haven't been able to call him Dad since he broke the news to me. I'm not sure that'll ever change, but times like these, I always seem to say it silently in my head. I might even squeeze him a little tighter, because I feel like such a shithead for leaving him alone again when he made me his whole world for eighteen years.

"I needed to get away for a little while," I say, my words muffled into his thick work coat.

We separate, and his eyes are misted. "Well, I'm glad as hell you're back. Not complaining, but you could have called and given me a heads-up. Things are kind of turned upside down right now."

He gestures to the materials littering the porch.

"What's this all about?" I wasn't expecting to see the farmhouse, let alone Edwin in it, upon my return. Everything on the farm should be flattened by now.

"Oh, just a little home-improvement project. June has been pecking at me about tuning things up in here. She wants to bring in a contractor, but the work keeps me busy, so I'm doing it myself, little by little."

I'm about to be outraged that she's putting Edwin to work remodeling a house he no longer owns. "Let me get this right. June Bell wants you to remodel *this* house?"

"She's got an opinion about everything these days. You'd think she lives here." He rolls his eyes and chuckles.

My eyes grow wide. My muscles tense. "She all but does. She owns the damn house. Now they're putting you to work on your way out the door?"

He frowns and laughs again. "No, Kase. It's not like that. Come on. You missed a lot."

He waves me in the front door, and I follow him into the kitchen.

"I guess so," I mutter, sizing up the construction debris on nearly every surface.

Paint cans are everywhere. The wooden trim has been stripped, along with the face of every cabinet in the room. At least the old pine floors have been refinished and given a generous coat of shine, restoring them to their original glory.

"Is there a home-improvement project you haven't started yet?"

He lifts an eyebrow and rubs the back of his neck as he looks around, surveying what can only be characterized as a midmakeover tornado.

"You know what they say. It has to get a whole lot worse before it gets better."

I meet his tentative look. "That sounds about right."

He cracks a smile and slaps my arm. "Lighten up, Kase. We'll get there. Maybe you can help me finish something before you disappear on us again."

I'm already mentally mapping out a to-do list, if only to minimize the number of power tools on the kitchen counters. Except I still don't understand why the hell he's bothering with all this.

He grabs a couple beers from the fridge and hands me one. "Come on. The back porch hasn't changed a bit. Promise."

I follow him out back, only to stop in my tracks one step outside. "Whoa."

Edwin stops at the rail, tips his bottle back and swallows. Together we stare out over the landscape of the farm. What I couldn't see from the road is clear now. Things *have* changed.

"What happened?"

"June took over. That's what happened. After you left, she and Gerald came here with a whole new plan. He didn't seem overly thrilled about it, but I think things happening the way they did maybe shocked him out of his usual pattern of thinking." He wrinkles his nose. "Shocked me out of it too, I suppose. She said it was time we let the past go and move on. And so we did."

"How does that explain the rest of this?"

"They reworked the blueprints from the expansion. I downsized the livestock and sold off some of the dairy operation to help fund the development. That, along with the loan from the Bells, was enough to get us started." He points to the north side of the property, where half a dozen little houses are framed and in various stages of completion. "We're starting with ten cottages that we can rent out year-round. As soon as they're up and running, the income will be enough to keep us going. That and all the crops she's planning."

"Crops?"

"We repurposed some of the fields for the development. We're switching up some of the others. June's got her head set on strawberries. She wants a whole damn field of them. She says the renters will love being able to pick their own. And she wants to expand on the orchard so we can get some more people coming here in the fall." He laughs. "You think *I've* got my hands full with projects. You should talk to her. She's unstoppable. Honestly, I think she's been bored out of her mind up at the hotel all these years, and she's finally getting to do something on her own. Bringing her here might have been the best thing you ever did for her."

I look at him again in disbelief.

He takes another swig of his beer and points to the cottages. "Go see for yourself. She's out there keeping everyone on their toes."

I ponder his suggestion a moment. The prospect of seeing her again has me frozen in place suddenly. Especially now that everything I believed to have happened has been all wrong. Now I hate myself for believing she'd let Edwin sell and turn my childhood home into ugly townhomes.

"I think I'll do that."

I leave the house, reeling. A second glance at Edwin's truck reveals the McCasker Farms logo retouched. No longer a faded blue, the lettering now frames two bright-red strawberries in the center. Relief like I've never known bubbles to the surface until I'm laughing and smiling ear-to-ear like an idiot.

How could I have ever underestimated her?

I drive toward the cottages, slowing by the custom-made sign that reads McCasker Farm Cottages.

I park in front of the first cottage, which seems near completion. Her Jeep is parked outside. She's here. My palms prickle with anxiety. I left her for four months. I never looked back. And I'm a repeat fucking offender. She's never going to forgive me for this.

But why would she do all this? Why would she save the farm if she didn't care?

I force myself out of the truck and up the front steps. I walk through the front door and she's there, standing across the room. Her arms are crossed. She's staring out a picture window facing the pasture and the mountains beyond. In this moment, she has no idea I'm here, and I almost wish I could be here a few more minutes to simply acclimate to being in her presence again without her knowing. Maybe build up the nerve to face the wrath I surely deserve.

I take a couple tentative steps forward. "That's quite the view," I say.

She spins toward me. Her arms fall to her sides and her face registers her shock. One look at her feels like blunt force to the chest. That hollow place where my heart used to be. Does she have any idea how empty I am without her?

I stop when we're only a few feet away from each other.

"Kase..." Her lip quivers.

God, she's beautiful. Her hair is a mess, a dull pencil poked through her bun. Her jeans and shoes are dusty. I just want to wrap my arms around her. I'm convinced I could simply hold her for hours, cherish her heartbeat, the feel of her breath, the smell of her skin.

"What are you doing here?"

I glance around and then back to her. "I was about to ask you the same question."

Her lips form a little *o*, and she follows my circuit around the room. "It's not what you think, Kase. We changed the plans."

"I know," I say quietly.

She exhales softly. "Oh."

"Why are you doing all this?"

She presses her lips together and turns away. "I'm just trying to make things right."

I step closer and touch her shoulder. She shivers. How I ache to lean in and bury my nose in her hair, taking her scent into me. Her taste. Her moans...

"June." I can hear my desperation in her name. The months of aching and missing her.

She wraps her arms around herself tightly, like she's hoping that can keep me out.

"I'm so sorry," I say quietly. "I wanted to give you time."

She swivels back around, her eyes narrow and misty. "Time? You think I haven't wasted enough of my life waiting for you to come back to Falls Edge for me? I didn't need time. I needed *you*, Kase. That's all I ever needed, and you left me here." She cuts herself off, bringing her fingertips to her shaking lips.

I work my jaw, trying to ignore how her words dig into me. I almost forgot how much the truth could hurt.

"I was afraid, all right? I ran. I couldn't stomach the thought of losing you and watching you slip away."

"I wasn't—"

"You left me first, okay? I know why you did. You were hurting, but my heart was in this too. I know I screwed up. I should have told you everything. I just..." I close my eyes and reach for the right words. "I've been broken for so long, June. And when you left, maybe I convinced myself I was foolish to believe we could have something so perfect. So right. That I could deserve you."

"I shouldn't have left you," she whispers, her eyes glimmering with unshed tears.

I pray that means it's not too late. I send up a solemn vow never to do anything so damn stupid as long as I live if she'll have me now. If she'll take me back.

"Tell me I'm not too late, June. Tell me I've still got a chance."

She laughs and brushes away the tear that falls. "My God, Kase. Do you know how long I've waited to be with you?"

"Probably just as long as I have. But I think we've run clean out of excuses, grudges, and tragedies to keep us apart, don't you? Time to get on with it already."

Her lips curve up into a sad smile, but I'm not convinced I've won her over. I hurt her. I dealt a blow that might take time to recover from. I'm ready to do the time, but hell, I need some hope right now.

Take me back. Take me back...

I want to drag her against me and kiss her until she gives in to me, but that's not enough. The answer has to come from her heart. I already know her body will say yes to what I want to give her, which is a lifetime supply of bliss and earth-shattering orgasms.

I'm on my knees before I know what I'm doing. I grab her hand and gaze up at her.

"Will you take me back?"

She shakes her head with a laugh. Then a sigh. And another smile, one that reaches her eyes. "I will take you back."

I grin broadly, like I've just won the world's best and biggest grand prize of all time. Another chance with the love of my life. And the thread I thought was unraveling everything just started making something new. A whole new dream I could have never imagined without June in my life.

"I may have one condition," she says. "Maybe two."

EPILOGUE

KASE

June wanted to move into the farmhouse as soon as I helped Edwin finish up the remodel. She was done living in a hotel suite, and she spent most of her days managing the cottage operation anyway. I couldn't think of a better arrangement, considering I'd never wanted her to leave in the first place.

I helped Edwin finish the dozen or so projects he'd started, and together we put the house back together. Spurred by a desire to satisfy June's wish and give our family a place to grow, we made the farmhouse livable again. Over those couple of months, all the blood, sweat, and tears seemed to heal what had been broken between Edwin and me. By the time we were putting on the finishing touches, the first cottage was complete. It turned out to be perfect for Edwin, who was already eager to help with odds and ends that came up once the rental operation was underway.

June refused to tell me what her second condition was until the farmhouse was ready.

She was moved in. We shared a closet, a toothbrush holder, and a towel rack. We even had a Christmas tree sitting in the living room, strung with hundreds of tiny white lights. Settled on the couch sipping her nightcap, she finally revealed the last, and final, condition to her taking me back for good.

I even had multiple choice. I could tattoo her name on my ass, or I could marry her. She wasn't about to let anyone in town think I was available. Not after the hell I'd already put her through. Twice.

Naturally, I was ready for anything that bound June Bell to me in the most permanent way possible.

★ ★ ★ ★

As soon as winter thawed and spring warmed into early summer days, we invited half of Falls Edge to witness our nuptials. We married at the hotel, of course. Gerald insisted on it, ensuring that everything was beautiful and perfect and expensive.

Halfway through the reception, a few slow dances and one locomotion later, June's bridal hairdo is coming undone. So is my patience, seeing her glowing in her pale-pink gown for hours on end. Layers upon layers of organza flow out from her sweetheart bodice, its beading sparkling like her eyes in the firelight. And the way she feels against me when we dance is pure heaven because she's my wife now, and I'm never letting her go again.

We sway together to a slow song, her body pressed snug to mine, her smile lighting up my heart like a night of the best fireworks ever.

"How are you feeling, Mrs. McCasker?"

Her eyes gleam with happiness. "Happier than I've ever been, my sweet husband."

I grin. "Oh, I'm not sweet at all."

"No?" She quirks an eyebrow.

"No, I'm downright devious. I can't believe you fell for that nice-guy routine this whole time."

She laughs and slaps my chest. "Don't you think you're smart?"

I wag my eyebrows, earning another musical laugh that makes me want to explode from pure joy.

Composing herself, she curls her lips into a coy smile. "What you don't know is that I have this thing for bad boys. I had you pegged this whole time. I've just been making you play nice so I could get my dream house before you turned into the devil I know you really are."

I shake my head and cluck my tongue. "Aren't you clever?"

She agrees with a curt nod before I lean in and brush a kiss to her soft pink lips.

"What *you* didn't know," I whisper, "is that I saw right through your little act. I knew under the innocent virgin I wanted to dirty up was a little sex kitten who would never be truly satisfied until she had a bad boy like me... A man who could put her on her knees and make her come like a rocket. All. Night. Long."

Her mirth fades, washed away by the passionate heat glinting in her eyes. No longer pink and sparkling, she's a dusty rose now. Her cheeks are flushed, and her skin shimmers like it does when she's incredibly turned on. Her palm is hot in mine, and I'm certain the entire room has just shot up at least twenty degrees. Tonight is our wedding night, and I have well-laid plans. I just thought I'd be able to wait until the guests left before my willpower totally vanished.

"You want to get out of here?"

I'm certain she can hear the animal need clawing at me with each inviting word. She seems to when she slides up against me, making me strongly consider pushing up her skirts and taking her right here. Right now.

Heaven help me, the things I'm going to do to this woman. Thank God I have a lifetime to work through the list.

I release her hand to pull a small folded piece of paper from my pocket. I slip it subtly between our palms as we continue to dance.

Her eyes brighten. "What is this?"

I grin, enjoying her curiosity and impatience. Both qualities make teasing her worth every ounce of restraint I have to exercise. I graze my hand across her back, over bare skin, before cinching our bodies tighter, making damn sure she can feel what she does to me.

She exhales softly, and I can tell she's as worked up as I am. She reaches for the note with the hand I'm not holding, but I extend our clasp away.

"You can read it later."

"I thought we were getting out of here," she says with breathy desire.

I exhale a groan and drag my nose along her neck, inhaling her perfume. "We are absolutely getting out of here. But if you move away from me right now, everyone's going to know that I've been thinking filthy things about my wife."

She smirks and flickers her gaze around the room as if she only now remembered we shared it with at least a hundred others.

"Okay, then we should think and *talk* about something else before the song ends."

"Hmm. That's all you. I'm a lost cause." I really am. June has bewitched me—body, mind, and soul—from the day she walked back into my life.

"I want pumpkins."

I tilt my head back, my eyes wide. "Pumpkins."

She nods. "It'll be great to have them in the fall."

"Woman." I sigh. She has had me on my toes planting new crops and changing things around for months. Patrons of the McCasker Farm will want for nothing, I swear.

She sifts her fingers through the hair at the nape of my neck, distracting me from mentally sorting out how and where I'm going to put her pumpkin patch. Because I'll give her whatever she wants, for as long as I'm breathing.

"All right, June. If you want pumpkins, I'll grow you pumpkins."

She smiles broadly. In an instant, all the work I've just committed myself to is instantly worth it.

"I found a recipe in Haidee's cookbook for pumpkin pie. I'll make you some the first chance I get."

"Sounds delicious," I say. Then I kiss her again, slowly, tenderly, and with only a fraction of the passion I plan on showing her later. "I may think of a few other ways for you to thank me too."

JUNE

When the song fades out, I make a bolt for the wedding party table while Kase wanders through the ballroom doors and out of sight. I don't know what he's up to, but I can't wait to find out.

I take a gulp of my water, because I'm parched and roughly a thousand degrees after that dance with Kase. My forever lover. My husband. I let a giddy smile take over. Knowing I'm officially married to the love of my life is so much more than a dream come true. It's a blessing I'll always cherish. A gift I'll always hope to reciprocate by giving my gorgeous husband more loving than he can handle.

With that in mind, I unfold the piece of paper in my hand and begin to read.

June Bell McCasker, queen of my heart...

By the time you read this, you'll already be my wife. We will have laughed, danced, and maybe even cried. I will have shared you with our friends and family, watching you glow like the beacon of pure happiness that you've become for me. We will have said our vows, but I will have wanted to say so much more. Because words will never be enough, I will have wanted to seal it with more than a kiss...

If you're reading this now, it means I can't wait another minute to steal you away. Meet me by the bridge in 20 minutes.

I love you.

Kase

Good God, how am I supposed to wait that long? I'm already bouncing in place, anxious and fidgety when Julie comes up to congratulate me. She's had so many glasses of champagne that she easily makes me forget the time with her rambling. Fifteen minutes later, not trying to seem too eager to break away from her tearful reminiscing about our friendship, I hug her tightly and disappear from the bustling ballroom as discreetly as I can.

Downstairs, the patio spans the width of the hotel. I hear an engine hum in the distance. I ditch my wedding shoes and run toward the sound. When I cross the bridge, Kase is there in a golf cart, a bottle of Dom between his thighs and two flutes in one hand.

"You look like you're up to no good," I say with a laugh. "Where did you get that?"

He smirks and shrugs. "I borrowed a bottle from the bar in Eve's. I'm sure your dad will forgive me." He extends his empty hand toward me. "And you look good enough to eat. Come on."

I climb into the cart with him without delay, because I'm all about no good right now. Kase had me pegged for sure.

I take the glasses from him so I can hold his hand as he drives. "Where are we going?"

"You'll see."

I'm bouncy and anxious when, a few minutes later, we're nearing the grove. The steady rush of the falls can be heard in the distance. My belly flutters with anticipation when we step off the cart, and Kase leads me toward the path up the falls lit by dozens of tiny tea lights.

My jaw falls in awe. "Kase."

He doesn't speak. He just guides me carefully up the smooth flat rocks until we're at the very place where he'd kissed me all those years ago.

He takes the glasses from me and sets the champagne aside before coming back to me. The clusters of lights at the top cast a glow over us, making the mist from the falls look like a million particles of fairy dust dancing in the air. He takes my hand and tugs me closer. I look up at him, breathless and more in love than I ever believed possible.

"This is incredible," I say.

Because in this moment, he's the old Kase, the mysterious boy I always wondered about—the one who chased me up the falls to kiss me the way he'd always wanted to, working his way into my heart so thoroughly that I had no choice but to wait for him to come back to me.

As if he's reading my every thought, he cradles my face in his palms. His eyes search mine. "This is when I knew," he says. "The minute I touched you, I knew you owned me."

I cover his hands with mine. "And now you own me too."

He bows his head until our foreheads touch. I can feel his shallow breaths, warmth mingling with the cool misty air.

"Thank you," he whispers. "For making every new day the best day of my life. For trusting me when I was too scared to trust anyone."

My heart is bursting. Aching with pure happiness. Unshed tears sting behind my eyes, but I've lasted all day without ruining my makeup. There's only one way I want to get messy, and that's with Kase, our bodies entwined, embedded, joined in perfect abandon.

"Kiss me, Kase. More than kiss me. Make me yours."

With my invitation, he crashes his lips to mine. No longer tender. No longer teasing and sweet. He leads a frenzy of desperate touches with his mouth, and then his palms feverishly seek more of my flesh. He walks us backward to where a couple of cushions and blankets are spread out. He'd come up here in anticipation of this moment, which makes me want it so much more.

He sits down, guides me so I straddle him, and wastes no time finding his way up my fluffy skirts.

"Fuck," he groans when his fingertips reach my bare sex.

A secretive smile curves my lips. "You didn't think I'd make an exception today, did you?" As soon as the negligée portion of the pre-wedding photos was over and the dress was in place, I'd quickly ditched the satiny panties, hoping that by the time the night was over, Kase would know I'd been this way all day, waiting for a moment just like this. "I wasn't about to let you ruin a beautiful pair of panties by tearing them off me like a savage."

"Oh, and I would have. They would have been shredded," he

rasps, sealing our mouths in another greedy kiss.

I don't have to beg or work his cock free from his tuxedo pants. He's ahead of me, moving quickly to spread me under my skirts and guide me down onto his length. He binds us one searing inch at a time before punching his hips up. Again and again, harder and deeper until my cries of ecstasy fill the night air. They're made of the sweetest satisfaction, the deepest love, and every ounce of gratitude that's collected inside me over the course of this incredible day.

"I love you. I love you so much," I say, winding my arms around him with no plans to ever let go.

"I love you, June. I will always love you."

KASE

A year and a half later...

I wake up from a nap and check the clock. It's well past noon, and for a split second, I'm in a panic that I'm late to milk the cows. But now that we've downsized the dairy operation, my time is dedicated to the fields. That and making my wife happy, one special project at a time. I spent the morning planting more bulbs in the backyard. In the spring they'll sprout up around an oak tree that June likes to sit under on sunny afternoons with her lunch.

She said my mother, wherever she is, probably would have loved that spot, looking over the pasture and the fields, the barns and rows of tiny white cottages. Even though it still hurts, the fact that she left and never came back, June's rekindled a little bit of hope that love exists inside the absence. Love and probably fear and regret. But mostly, hopefully, an enduring love. Wherever my mother is, I hope she knows we've made a home for her memory.

I pour a cup of coffee and go out onto the back porch to survey the fruits of my labors again. In the distance, June is walking up from the field, holding an enormous pumpkin to her hip.

"Goddamnit."

I put my coffee down and sprint to meet her. I'm out of breath when I get to her.

"What in the hell do you think you're doing?"

I scoop the pumpkin away from her and she sighs with relief instantly. "Thanks, honey. I found the perfect one, and I knew I'd never find it again in the patch, so I just had to bring it home."

"Baby, you cannot be carrying twenty-pound pumpkins across fields. You're carrying enough as it is." I caress over the swell of her belly and lean down to kiss her forehead. She smells like the field. Like fresh country air and fall leaves, all the things our guests come to Falls Edge to experience on their weekends away from the city.

She tilts her head up and finds my lips, pressing herself into me even though her belly keeps us from getting as close as we once were. Being eight months pregnant with our son hasn't slowed her down from moving or fussing or working just as much as she used to—a fact that bewilders and infuriates me at times.

"Come on," I say, taking her hand. "You should get off your feet."

She frowns. "I'm fine, Kase. Seriously. Plus, I still need to make those apple pies for the farmers market tomorrow."

I roll my eyes. "I'll make the pies. You can give me instructions."

She huffs out a sigh but doesn't argue. I smile, because for now I've got my way. We walk together toward the house. The oak tree and the lilies and the back-porch swing come into clear view. Beyond, the mountains in all their quiet wonder frame the picture of our home. In that moment, with my wife by my side, carrying my future inside her, I know without a doubt that all my dreams have come true.

ALSO AVAILABLE FROM
WATERHOUSE PRESS

Keep reading for an excerpt!

CHAPTER ONE

MADISON

Pop!

My heart leaps at the sound. A rush of fizz pours from the top of the champagne bottle, dousing my hands. I curse inwardly and mop the mess off the counter. Not bothering with a glass, I take the bottle with me to the couch and curl up for another quiet night in. I flip through the channels and settle on a made-for-TV movie. All I need is a pint of Ben & Jerry's to complete my look as a miserable divorcée.

I thought when all the paperwork was finalized today, something would change... *I* would change. I was no longer Madison Cleary, the wife on the arm of a rising star. I was officially Madison Atwood again. The new Madison should feel happy and relieved and free. But something about this celebration feels so incredibly empty.

I close my eyes and exhale a tired sigh.

Goddamn him. As hard as I try, I can't seem to let go of my anger.

Rejection. Hope. Failure. Determination. Yes...determination is here and fighting for ground too.

I put the bottle down and reach for my laptop. The Internet

has answers and surely this isn't the end for me. The failure of my marriage has been a devastating blow, without a doubt. But I can't let my famous and infamously unfaithful husband—*ex-husband*—jeopardize my future.

Sometimes it feels like he's everywhere, though. Clients, gigs, and friends still exist in our shared circles. If I ever want to feel completely myself again, I need a break. I need to get away from LA, the whispers, and the chapter of my life that I'd just signed into the past.

A trip to Baja, maybe. Meet a sexy, rich producer who would blacklist the fucker I'd stood by so faithfully through his rise to fame. We'd sip expensive champagne and eat just enough decadent food to fuel our back-to-back sexcapades. And of course we'd kill time in between by frolicking in the clear blue ocean.

I let that fantasy play out for a few minutes before tugging my thoughts back to reality, or at least a more realistic getaway. The last few months of marriage to Jeremy and the subsequent months negotiating our divorce had produced the most anguished dry spell I had experienced since high school. Jeremy and I had met as naïve, fumbling teenagers. We'd been together ever since. I'd been stupid in love with him then.

The memory hits me, but the pain hits me harder—deep in my gut, before it travels up my esophagus causing a painful burn. All those memories are tainted now, and I hate him for that more than anything.

Maybe it won't always be this way. Maybe one day I'll heal. He'll be a memory, but a distant one. I won't always feel this way...

Emotionally charged, I start a new search for spa retreats. As much as I wish I could fuck the feelings away on a tropical island with a beautiful stranger, I know no good will come from that. I need a real break. Something restorative. Something that can heal all the tears in my heart.

The first few search results return locations in northern California. Far enough from LA, but close enough that I could come back for work in a pinch. I click through website after website. The options are either too dated, too crunchy, or tout a brand of spirituality I'm not ready for. I don't want to be converted. I just need some quiet time, maybe a few massages, and some fresh mountain air.

Pure determination brings me to the second page of results. I click on the website for Avalon Springs Retreat. My heart lifts and brings some hope up with it. Avalon Springs is basically a spa in the mountains. Home-cooked meals, yoga classes, a few outdoor excursions, and big blocks of time meant to help people re-center. The owners look like legit hippies. The accommodations appear clean and comfortable. And it doesn't seem like a convoluted tourist trap for the prima donnas I'm hoping to take a break from.

I check my schedule, ignore the pricing—because I deserve this no matter the cost—and book a four-week stay.

Today I am Madison Atwood, and the next chapter of my life is going to start at Avalon Springs.

★ ★ ★ ★

"Here's your room key. You have a king suite in the Olive Annex, which is that way. It's only the next building over, so you're not far from the dining room and the classes." The young girl with flawless skin and thick blond dreads points to the front entrance of the retreat. "Every Saturday we do an orientation session here in the main house. That'll start in about an hour."

"An orientation?" I lift my gaze from the paper nametag where *Indigo* is written in sloppy script to her pale gray eyes.

She smiles loosely, as if she hasn't experienced an ounce of tension in her life. "Yeah. It's kind of like a meet and greet. You'll introduce yourself to the other residents, do some breathing exercises and stretching, and Vi and Lou will talk a little bit more about the springs."

"Great," I mutter, not bothering to disguise my lack of enthusiasm. I doubt this easy-breezy flower child will pick up on it anyway.

I tuck the cool metal key into my back pocket, a small sign of my commitment to this getaway that I already fear is a complete and utter mistake. The reception area is noisy as a pack of people linger outside what appears to be a yoga class. Or maybe it's the beginning of the orientation gathering. Anxiety hits and the familiar burn in my stomach follows.

There is nothing quiet about this. Nothing restorative. Sure, this is a definite break from the city scene, but these are *not my people.* I can rub shoulders with Hollywood's rich and famous, but five minutes with this enlightened collective is sending me into a tailspin.

I cut Indigo off before she can finish her intro speech, grab the check-in paperwork, and head out the front door a lot faster than I came through it. The journey from my Beamer to my room is mercifully short, although I'm not thrilled to be staying so close to the epicenter of this "quiet mountainside retreat."

I send up a tiny prayer of thanks that at least the room delivers. It's all as advertised—clean, cozy, and spacious. After a quick tour of the room's amenities, I peek out the window to see what or who is making the noise. A stream of apparently eager "residents" are filing into the main building. Yoga pants and head bands seem to be the uniform. I stare down at my outfit—torn jeans, a tight V-neck, and a pair of well-loved Chucks.

Decidedly out of my element, I grab my key and the map of the property that I'd all but torn out of Indigo's hand and head out. I walk briskly past the small crowd and keep moving until they are only a quiet murmur of activity behind me.

The landscape here is different than anything I'm used to. I'd been an East Coast girl all my life, always working on my career, and—once we came out west—*his* career, so I rarely made it to the more scenic places in California.

As I follow a wide, worn path that weaves into denser areas, my thoughts are loud. Doubt. Regret. Hopelessness. They shout and cling to me. If I walked into that orientation right now, I'd be wearing it all over me. I'd be a beacon of not belonging. That lost woman whose husband left her because she wasn't the quintessential arm candy he needed her to be. The rejection and the pain feel like a big, ugly tattoo that no amount of time will ever be able to wear off.

I push myself farther, vaguely noting the incline and the fine sheen of perspiration that beads on my skin as I go. Maybe Avalon Springs isn't the haven I truly need. But I've come this far...

Tears burn behind my eyes because I'm alone. So utterly alone.

Clusters of pines hug the trail. Above the treetops, the sky is a majestic shade of purple. My thoughts quiet enough for me to realize that despite being well away from the retreat center now, night is coming on and I have no idea where I am or where I'm going. But the faint sound of water lures me forward.

Beyond the trees is a clearing, a well of water at its center. Despite the cooler temperature at this elevation, steam swirls off the vibrant turquoise pool. I scale a smooth, round rock and test the temperature of the water with my fingertips. Perfect, like a freshly drawn bath.

This must be *the* Avalon Springs. The retreat's namesake promises healing properties from the mineral deposits that run off the nearby mountains. Rivulets of water trail off higher rocks and down into nature's most perfect bath tub.

After taking a quick glance around, I act. I strip my clothes and dip my naked toes into the water. Then, with care, I submerge my body. I let my head slip underwater, and my hair swirls like a thousand strands of silk around my bare shoulders. I groan with relief and bubbles float through the clear water to the surface. I take turns swimming and sinking my whole body deep into the water. The heat and the water, being unburdened of my clothes and all those heavy thoughts... Nothing has ever felt so good.

My toes find the bottom, and I launch myself back to the surface when I need air. After a while I wade to a place where I can easily stand. My breasts hover just above the surface of the water. I pull myself onto a wide, flat rock that frames the pool and lie on it, unbothered that it's both hard and cool against my skin. I'm warm and relaxed from my swim in the springs.

I close my eyes, enjoying the simple sounds of water and birds and the isolation that I'd hiked all this way to find. I skim my hands over my skin, and for the first time in what seems like forever, I notice a faint pulse between my thighs. God, I'm strung so tight lately. So in need of release. Encouraged that my body is still paying attention to some of my basic needs, I touch and tease myself to a higher point of arousal.

Getting close, I spread my thighs and dip a finger into my pussy while the other plays my clit like a record. Minutes pass as I deftly manipulate the places that ache for the attention of a man. And not just any man. One who won't break me all over again. I don't have one of those, so for now, my touch will have to do.

My breathing ticks up with my pace. I've brought myself to this point a thousand times. I know just what to do. More times than not, though, the act leaves me feeling empty. Physically satisfied, but never emotionally. I don't care. After the five-hour drive from the city, I need a release. I curve my fingers deeper into my pussy and graze the tips rhythmically across the rough pad of skin inside. The soft head of a man's engorged cock would feel better there, but whatever.

I lick my lips and imagine a man is pleasing me right now. Thick and brawny, passion in his eyes, he's filling me with every inch of his silky cock. He's telling me I'm beautiful, that I feel better than anyone he's ever had. He's grazing over that magic spot, over...and over...and...

With a sharp inhale, I bow off the rock, so close, so ready. My heels and shoulder blades press hard against the rock. I release a cry that's half arousal and half frustration, because the orgasm is just beyond reach.

I open my eyes. Stars puncture the navy sky with tiny pinpricks of light. I glance back to the trail and push down a flash of worry that I might not be able to find my way back.

Then I see him through the trees. And I scream.

LUKE

I'm not sure what possessed me to stop and watch her. She'd been loud enough marching up the path. Another city girl passing through the retreat at the base of the mountain, no doubt. I'd come here tonight to enjoy the springs because Saturday is their turnover day and the new residents rarely venture up past sunset.

But the second this woman's clothes hit the ground, I couldn't move. I should have made my way back to my cabin up the mountainside, but instead I watched her swim and float like a goddess through the water. She had long brown hair that clung in a straight slick v down her back when she rose above the water, revealing possibly the most perfect set of breasts I'd ever seen on a woman.

And then, with only a little guilt, I watched her slide up on that rock and plunge her slender fingers into her pussy until her cries echoed off the rocks and rendered the forest and my breathing silent. Now I'm hard, in absolutely no condition to comfortably return home. And I can't in good conscience leave her up here as night quickly falls around us.

When our eyes lock, she screams and slips back into the water to hide her nakedness. I adjust myself enough to disguise how her little display has affected me and walk closer.

"Who are you?" Her voice is shaky with panic. She stares at me wide-eyed, probably contemplating if I'm going to do her any harm.

At this hour, this far from the retreat, she is wise to worry. Nothing could protect her from someone of my size and skillset if I had malicious intentions.

"I'm not going to hurt you," I offer gently, hoping to ease her fears. "You're out here pretty late. Do you know your way back?"

She folds her arms over her chest, even though I can't see anything under the water anyway.

"I have a map."

I smirk and glance briefly at the pile of clothes she'd abandoned for the springs. "Yeah? Do you have a flashlight to read the map?"

Grooves mark the space between her dark winged brows. Her eyes are stunning in their shape and intensity, even if I can't place the precise color in the fading light.

"I can take you back. Someone like you shouldn't be out here alone."

Her frown deepens. "Someone like me?"

"You're at least a mile from the retreat. You have no supplies and no provisions. Someone without a healthy fear of the wild outdoors, at this hour or any other, shouldn't be out here alone."

"I don't need rescuing, okay?"

I resist the urge to roll my eyes. Another asshole from the city with too much ego and not enough sense. "Let's go. I'll take you back."

Slowly she moves to the edge toward her clothes, never taking her eyes off me. "Look away, please."

I laugh. "I've seen a lot more than you're about to show me."

Her eyes widened and her nostrils flare. Without another word, I turn casually to give her privacy that seems pointless after what I just witnessed. A minute later, the sound of her sneakers scraping against the rock prompts me to turn. She is fully dressed, and I allow myself a moment to appreciate her body with clothes on. Her jeans hug her thighs nicely, and her breasts look fuller in the tight shirt.

I dislodge the thoughts around that assessment before my cock starts misbehaving again. I haven't been with a woman in a long time, and even though I despise everything this one probably stands for, I can't help that the beast in me wants to tear her clothes off and bury myself inside her until we both come. Repeatedly.

I mutter a curse under my breath before turning and heading swiftly down the path.

A few minutes pass and I don't need to look back. I hear ragged breathing and branches cracking under her careful footing—signs she is struggling to keep up. She has no business in the woods. Why Lou and Vi keep luring these idiots to this beautiful place is beyond me. People like her will never belong here. They'll never appreciate this place the way they should. A week in the mountains is a fashion statement for most of these people, and I just want them out of my woods and off my mountain so I can enjoy what I came here for. Solitude. Peace. A simple life. A quiet dip in the springs without some sexy little city girl cluttering up my thoughts with her sweet pussy...because I'm pretty sure it's sweet, and oh so tight.

I halt in my tracks and spin. The brunette nearly barrels into me. I catch her by the shoulders when she tips off balance. Somehow she feels smaller in my arms, just a little bit of flesh covering the delicate structure of her frame. Her wet hair dampens her shirt, drawing my attention to that lovely rack again. Goddamn, this woman is a distraction I didn't ask for.

"You can get there from here," I say gruffly.

Her eyes go wide again. "I can?"

The moonlight glints on her skin. If she'd worn makeup, the springs had washed it away, leaving her natural and bare. She's definitely pretty. A pert nose and a little bow of a mouth. There's nothing exotic or stark about her features, but she's someone who looks perfectly gorgeous with no effort.

I release my hold on her and jab my thumb in the direction behind me. "It's just a few yards down the path. You'll see the lights, and they will lead you the rest of the way."

"Thank you," she says softly, almost too softly to hear if not for the near silence of the woods at night. Gone is the tone she'd given me earlier. How she'd gone from rapture to claiming that she didn't need rescuing, I didn't know. But maybe that had been fear talking.

I wince, because I don't like the idea of being feared. I'd never hurt her, or anyone. Even if I didn't want them in my woods. "You don't have to thank me."

"Yes, I do. You could have left me there, or..."

"Or?" I lift an eyebrow, challenging her to say it out loud.

True enough, I could have done all the things I couldn't stop thinking about right now. I could have gotten myself between her silky thighs, plunged into her, stretched her pussy around me, and satisfied her in ways those pretty little fingers never would.

But she doesn't say any of that. She doesn't say a word. She only gazes up at me, and for a second I wonder if she can read my thoughts, if somehow this unexpected depravity radiates off me. Then her hands slide up the front of my chest, and I almost forget how to breathe.

"What's your name?" Her voice is a whisper now, like she's hiding from her own words.

When had a woman touched me last? I can't fucking breathe.

"Good night."

I push past her, forcing my legs to move me back up the trail. I have to get the hell away from her.

CHAPTER TWO

MADISON

What the hell was that? I asked him a simple question and he stalked off like a savage without so much as a response. He dismissed me like I was the one who'd intruded on his private moment, not the other way around.

Fueled by anger, I make my way down the trail toward the main house, following the light just as he told me. My legs ache, the strain from the hike making each step feel like it may be my last.

Leaning forward, I rest my hands on my knees, giving myself a moment to catch my breath. All I can think about is him—the sexy stranger who came out of nowhere and, although he'd watched me, hadn't wanted to engage.

The lights from the expansive windows spanning the back of the lodge illuminate the clearing only a dozen yards in front of me. Pushing off my knees, I propel myself forward to the only place I want to be—my room.

I take a few steps and the memory of touching him stops me. *Oh God.* I touched him too. Why did I do that? Maybe I misread the look in his eyes before I slid my hand up the front of his chest. The hard muscles underneath my palm felt like steel. He brushed past me and disappeared like I'd offended him in some way.

As I break through the brush and reach the clearing, I see Indigo standing on the wraparound wooden deck, staring off into space.

When she spots me, she waves frantically. "Oh my God, Ms. Atwood! We were looking for you."

I climb the steps slowly and hold onto the railing to keep my balance. "I didn't mean to be gone so long."

"I almost sent out the search party when you weren't in your room and didn't show up at orientation."

"Sorry." I'm not being sincere. The last thing I wanted to do tonight was go to an orientation. I came here to be alone and get away from it all. Not be surrounded by strangers and follow a schedule.

"It's okay. I made you an appointment with Vi tomorrow." She smiles brightly, coming to my side when I finally make it to the main level. "She's going to give you a private tour of the property. It's very important to us that our guests have the best experience possible."

"Uh, thanks." My lack of enthusiasm is evident in my voice, but when her smile fades I try to recover. "I appreciate you looking after me, Indigo."

She places her hand on my arm and gives it a light squeeze. "We're only trying to help."

"I know. It's just been a long day."

"Well," she says filled with excitement, "I can make you a nice cup of cocoa to help you relax."

"No." My refusal comes a little too fast, but I've hit my limit of happy people for today. "I just need a bath and some sleep. I appreciate the offer though. It's very kind of you."

"All part of the job. If you change your mind, we're going to be having a campfire starting around nine down there." She motions to the right side of the clearing where a man is throwing logs into a pit and another is rearranging chairs in a circle. "Stop by maybe. It always helps me sleep."

I have a feeling that nothing has kept her up a night in her life. There's a lightness to Indigo that I wish I could feel again. Something I'm sure I had in my youth, before reality slapped me in the face. "Night, Indigo." I smile softly.

"Night, Ms. Atwood. Sleep tight."

Restful sleep has eluded me since news of Jeremy's infidelity graced every gossip rag in town. Some of the more serious news outlets even picked up the story, making the affair inescapable. The incessant phone calls and text messages had kept me awake and unable to move on from the heartbreak with the constant reminder of how I'd been wronged.

After I make my way to my room and take a shower, I crawl under the covers and stare up at the ceiling. No matter how hard I try, sleep escapes me. The only thing I can think about is the mysterious man in the woods. The asshole who brushed me off. The one I wanted to touch again. What would his bare chest feel like against my palms?

"Fuck." I hiss and slam my hands against the mattress.

I should be pissed at him for watching me, but remembering the look in his eyes when I caught him turns me on. No one has looked at me like that in ages. Living in LA does little for a woman's ego. Girls barely out of high school are all the rage and everyone else is getting plastic surgery to look more youthful than they really are.

But he looked at me with pure lust, the same way Jeremy did

before he strayed. The mystery man may have stalked off, but I know that he wanted me in that moment. Feeling the familiar, dull ache between my legs, I reach under the covers and touch myself. My eyes seal shut and images of the handsome, mysterious man flood my mind.

Something about his beauty... His eyes were hooded and rivaled the darkest night sky. Though his eyes were striking, his hair surprised me the most. The dirty blond streaks in his long wild hair matched the honey, tanned skin on his face. Even pulled back into a messy man bun, the look worked for him. His beard, something I'd never found attractive on a man, made his features more pronounced and impossibly more manly.

Picking up where I left off in the springs, I pretend instead of my own fingers, he is pounding into me. There's hunger in his eyes as he moans my name. He glides his rugged hands across my skin, scorching my flesh in their wake. I dig my heels into his ass, feeling the clench of his muscles with each pump. I'm unable to control my voice, my moans growing louder with each stroke.

The orgasm that eluded me earlier hits me hard now. I cry out, working my fingers in and out while rubbing my palm against my clit. My muscles tense as the waves of pleasure crash over me repeatedly and my body twists to one side. When the final crest crashes down, my eyes fly open and I gasp for air.

"Huh," I mutter on an exhale, still trying to catch my breath. Never in my life have I come so quickly. Not even after Jeremy spent so much time working me up that I couldn't even see straight. Even then, it took me at least ten minutes to reach an orgasm that was anything close to earth shattering. But this one, thinking of *him,* rocked my fucking world.

I'm too exhausted to overanalyze the situation. Closing my eyes, I try to clear my mind and focus on the crickets chirping outside my window. But it's no use. All I see is him.

LUKE

The last thing I expected last night was a naked woman, alone, pleasuring herself at the springs. Orientation day at Avalon should've been my time to enjoy that slice of the property without worry.

My grandfather left me the land—over fifty acres of pristine, secluded mountaintop in Northern California. I never planned to make it my home. The site sat abandoned for years with the cabin falling into disrepair. But when my last tour of duty ended, the thought of going back to my old life and being part of civilian society sent me into a tailspin.

Instead, I put my blood, sweat, and tears into this place and made it my home.

This was supposed to be my escape.

My haven from the outside world.

Until *she* showed up.

I sit and stare into the fire while I sip my morning coffee. I can't stop picturing the way her chestnut hair, dampened and wild, clung to her clothing, outlining her breasts. Her perfect breasts. Her perky breasts. Her plump breasts. *Think about something else, dumbass.* The last time I touched a pair was... Hell, it's been years.

Before joining the Navy, I'd had dreams of a normal life. None of them involved living in the woods, high up on a mountain, alone. I always thought I'd have the American dream—get married, buy a house, and fill it with so many kids I'd eventually end up driving a shitty minivan.

But my time in the military fucked that up. I thought I was prepared for whatever I was going to experience during my enlistment. I'd seen and done things I didn't want to relive or repeat, but I didn't have any issues coping until my last tour of duty. There didn't seem to be any rhyme or reason to our assignments. The violence seemed senseless.

By the time I was discharged as a decorated Navy SEAL, I couldn't imagine going back to "normal" life. My PTSD was so severe that even the sound of a car backfiring set me off. The only cure was self-imposed isolation.

I can function around people if I need to. Every now and again I venture into town but never stay long. I know the way everyone else lives, but that's not my world anymore. I'm better off alone. I prefer the peacefulness of my mountain.

Typically, my daily chores keep me occupied enough that my mind doesn't wander. But today all I can think of is the brown-haired beauty with her soft moans and killer tits. I should've left as soon as I laid eyes on her, but something about the way the moon glistened off her damp skin kept me glued to the spot. When she cried out, I lost all ability to think straight.

When she saw me, there was nothing but fear in her eyes. I'd seen that look a million times when I served in the military. I couldn't take the weight of it again. I couldn't leave without easing her mind and trying to satisfy my own conscience. I would never hurt her. Violence wasn't my style or in my nature. I'd sworn to serve and protect, not attack and scare.

But...I couldn't deny wanting to lean forward and press my body against hers... Plunge my tongue deep into her mouth. When she touched me, I'd wanted to act upon the fantasy, but then reality set in.

How could she be so frightened one minute and touching me the next? She had looked like she wanted me to kiss her... Of course I did the only thing that felt right—I ran.

The contact had shocked me.

Completely rocked me to my core.

Like a fucking asshole I turned my back on her, leaving her to fend for herself. I shouldn't have left her, but I didn't ask for company. *Fuck.* If she didn't make it back, Vi, Lou, and an entire search party would be canvassing the area, looking for her. I groan into my mug and regret leaving her to find her own way back. But it's been over ten hours and no one has knocked on my door. The likelihood that she survived is pretty high, right?

Over the next ten minutes, I push her out of my thoughts and make a mental list of the chores I have to get done today. Living the way I do takes planning, time, and most of all, effort. I don't run to the store for groceries. I grow my own food and raise my own livestock. Something as simple as heating my cabin has to be done by my hands. I spend hours a day chopping wood so when winter hits I'll have enough to get me through the season.

I toss my coffee cup in the sink and stare out the window that faces Avalon. It's a tiny speck in the distance, but it reminds me of her. When a fantasy of her moaning my name starts to take hold, I shake the thought from my head.

"Get a grip, Luke," I say. She's invaded my thoughts enough.

I head out into the crisp morning air, feed the chickens and other animals, and start on my daily task of splitting wood. The last thing I want is to be idle.

Sexual frustration courses through my veins, barely waning with every strike of the axe. I grip the handle tighter, swinging harder as she flashes through my mind. Images of her naked and the sounds of her moaning flood me like a seductive slide presentation only my sex-deprived mind could dream up.

Turning my face toward the sun, I wipe away the sweat that's starting to trickle down my temples. I silently curse my body and the woman who has worked her way inside my head. Even with my flannel unbuttoned, the cool morning air feels like a furnace blowing across my skin. Everything about my body is alive and burning with desire. My cock has stiffened to the point that I can barely think straight. Something has to be done about it before I end up cutting off my leg because I'm so fucking distracted.

I throw down the axe and stalk toward the cabin. I kick off my jeans and leave them on the bearskin rug in front of the fire before collapsing with a huff into my favorite chair. I grip my cock roughly. I give it a squeeze to settle it down and quench the dull ache that's plagued me since last night.

I lift my hips, chasing my hand with each stroke. The orgasm inside me builds with each pump of my fist. To get me there faster, I close my eyes and picture the moonlight sparkling off her naked flesh like a thousand diamonds set ablaze. I need this. I want this. I can almost feel her mouth wrap around the tip of my cock, languidly licking it as she moans in appreciation.

I grip hard. Pump faster. Straining to reach the orgasm that's just out of my grasp. Every time I get near, it eludes me. A tease within me—just like her.

"Hello," a voice says.

My heart stops, slamming against my chest like a truck hitting a brick wall at full speed.

My eyes fly open, and what do I see?

The object of my desire.

This story continues in *Misadventures of a City Girl!*

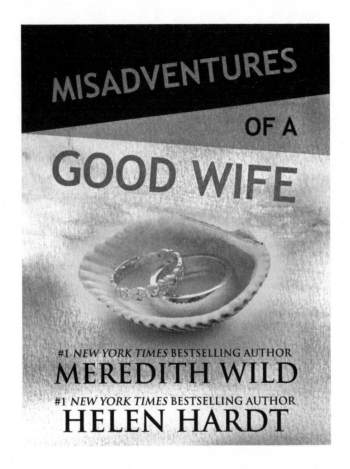

CHAPTER ONE

KATE

He always said I had the most beautiful blue eyes he'd ever seen.

In truth, my eyes were more gray than blue, but when he looked into them, his face between my thighs, his own eyes searing in their dark intensity, I believed my eyes were blue and beautiful.

"You like that, sweetness?" His words whispered across my wet skin, sending chills through me.

Price always looked into my eyes when he went down on me. He had from the very first time we'd made love back in college. Ours had been a whirlwind romance—love at first sight, as corny as that sounds. After graduation, he'd begun his job as a day trader on Wall Street, and I'd started as a copywriter for The New York Tribune. With luck, we'd happened upon our quaint Brooklyn apartment— cozy and perfect.

Yes, perfect.

Perfect was how I felt every time Price licked me there, tugging on me, his low growls reverberating against the sensitive skin of my inner thighs.

And his eyes never left mine.

"God, yes," I sighed. "Yes, yes."

He flipped me over onto my hands and knees and gave one cheek of my ass a little slap.

"You have the best ass, Kate."

Shivers surged through my body. I loved it when he sucked me in this position. Already, I was on the verge. I knew it wouldn't be long until he—

"Oh!"

Two of his fingers breached my wet channel, and the convulsions began. Price had given me countless orgasms over our years together, and each one always seemed more magnificent than the last. This one was an implosion—every cell in my body coursing toward my inner core. I pushed backward, trying to force his fingers farther and deeper into me.

"That's right. Come for me, sweet Kate."

My limbs shook, my arms finally giving way until only my thighs held my ass in the air.

"I love making you come," Price said, his voice low and husky. "Do you have any idea how beautiful you look right now?"

His words made me spiral toward the peak once more.

"I can feel you, sweetness. I feel you getting ready to come again." He removed his fingers, and in an instant he was inside me.

That's all it took. I exploded around him.

"Price! My God, Price!"

"That's it, baby. I love it when you scream my name. I love to make you come." He thrust once more. "You hug me so completely, Kate. No one else... No one else in the world but you..."

I pushed my hips backward, forcing him to increase his rhythm.

but I was exhausted. I'd pulled an eighty-hour week and still managed to get home to see Price before he left. Tomorrow was Saturday. I was going to indulge in a well-deserved session of sleeping in followed by a late lunch with my bestie and then a massage.

"Love you, baby," I said, drifting off.

His words echoed back to me. "And I love you. Always."

★ ★ ★ ★

I shot up in bed. What the hell was that annoying noise?

Not my alarm. I hadn't set it. I'd only lain down for an afternoon nap.

The door buzzer. I'd been so sound asleep that I hadn't recognized the ring. I quickly grabbed my phone off the night table. Noon? Damn. I'd really been exhausted. A wave of regret swept over me. I'd wanted to say goodbye to Price when he left. He was no doubt somewhere over the Atlantic by now.

I hurried into some sweats and a shirt and stumbled out of the bedroom to the front door. I opened the intercom. "Yes?"

"Mrs. Lewis? Katherine Lewis?"

I cleared my throat. "Yes."

"I'm Officer Trent Nixon, NYPD. I have...news for you. May I come up?"

My heart fell into my stomach.

Something was terribly wrong.

This story continues in *Misadventures of a Good Wife!*

Hard and fast. That's how I liked it, especially right before he left on one of his trips. He always made sure I'd think only of him while he was gone.

And I always did. He never left my thoughts.

He plunged into me more deeply and then withdrew. Though I whimpered at the loss, he flipped me over onto my back, spread my legs, and then tunneled into me.

"Look at me, Kate. I want to look into your beautiful blue eyes." Beads of sweat emerged on his brow, gluing dark strands of hair to his forehand. "You're beautiful. So beautiful." He thrust once more, groaning. "God, yeah. Feels so good."

So sensitive was I from my multiple orgasms, I felt every tiny convulsion as Price shot into me.

One day we'd make a baby together. The time wasn't right yet, but one day...

He collapsed on top of me, his body hot and slick. After a few seconds, he mumbled, "Sorry, baby," and moved to the side.

I turned toward him and brushed my lips over his. "I miss you already."

His arm was over his forehead, his eyes closed. "Me too. But it's only for a week."

I smiled and kissed him again. "A week sounds like a year to me."

He opened his eyes and turned toward me. "I know. I'll call you every day like I always do." Then he sighed. "I'd better get moving if I'm going to make that flight. An afternoon nap is just what you need. You deserve it."

The bed shifted as he got up. I wanted to stay awake until he left,

ABOUT MEREDITH WILD

Meredith Wild is a #1 *New York Times, USA Today,* and international bestselling author of romance. Living on Florida's Gulf Coast with her husband and three children, she refers to herself as a techie, whiskey-appreciator, and hopeless romantic. She has been featured on *CBS This Morning, The Today Show,* the *New York Times, The Hollywood Reporter, Publishers Weekly,* and *The Examiner.*

VISIT HER AT MEREDITHWILD.COM!

MORE MISADVENTURES

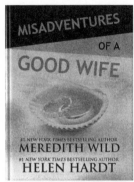

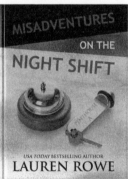

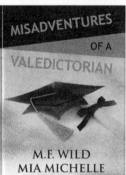

VISIT MISADVENTURES.COM
FOR MORE INFORMATION!

MORE MISADVENTURES

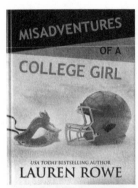

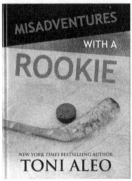

VISIT MISADVENTURES.COM
FOR MORE INFORMATION!